## "I am not in the habit of picking up men!"

"No, no, of course not," Mr. Rijnma ter Salis replied with infuriating calm. "But you're a beautiful woman, Eugenie, in a foreign country with no knowledge of the language and you are—forgive me for saying so—innocent."

"What utter rubbish!" she said tartly. "I can take care of myself. If you think that of me, I can't think why you offered me this job!"

Dear Reader,

I had been spending a day on Dartmoor and as usual allowed myself to dream about the people living there in their remote villages. Eugenie popped into my head at once: sensible, pretty and kind and not afraid of hard work—and at times a tart tongue. She had no idea what lay in store for her—nor, for that matter, had I. Mr. Rijnma ter Salis was inevitable, driving along the Dartmoor roads before I could stop him. And after that, they wove themselves into the story with very little daydreaming from me. Not knowing what they would be doing on the next page kept me writing furiously until the end. And I was sorry when I reached it.

*Betty Neels*

# A SECRET INFATUATION
## Betty Neels

# *Harlequin Books*

TORONTO • NEW YORK • LONDON
AMSTERDAM • PARIS • SYDNEY • HAMBURG
STOCKHOLM • ATHENS • TOKYO • MILAN
MADRID • WARSAW • BUDAPEST • AUCKLAND

ISBN 0-373-03363-X

A SECRET INFATUATION

Copyright © 1994 by Betty Neels.

First North American Publication 1995.

# CHAPTER ONE

EUGENIE SPENCER, tall, splendidly built, dark hair, dark eyes and beautiful, put out a reluctant hand to turn off the alarm clock and got out of her bed. She dug her feet into slippers, dragged on a dressing-gown and went to the window and peered out into the early day. The April morning was misty, veiling the moorland and the great outcrops of rock, although the mist was slowly dispersing under the faint warmth of the early sun. She nodded in satisfaction. Driving her father to Exeter would be no problem; she could take the Moretonhampstead road across the moor. It was lonely for most of the way but she had been born and brought up on Dartmoor and was familiar with its vastness, its sudden mists and wild winter weather. Her father had been team rector for as long as she could remember, visiting the remote villages over a wide area, assisted by two fellow clergy. When she had gone away to train as a nurse and then take a post as ward sister at a London teaching hospital, she had returned home at every opportunity until his sudden severe heart attack had put an end to her career; for, after several weeks of hospital treatment, it was obvious that he wouldn't be fit for work for a long time. He was sent home to recover slowly and she had given up her job and come home to help her mother, take upon her shoulders the mundane parochial jobs, nurse her father and cope with the Reverend Mr Watts who had been sent to act as locum to the parish. A zealous young man who, coming from one of the big inner cities, had no idea of village life and even less of village life on Dartmoor.

The villages were small and widely scattered, not to mention the remote farmhouses, frequently cut off in winter. This morning, though, the moor was inviting, stretching away in grand loneliness as far as the eye could see. Eugenie nipped smartly across the landing to the bathroom to begin her day.

Presently, in a tweed skirt, a sweater over a blouse and sensible shoes on her feet, her hair piled rather haphazardly on top of her head, she went downstairs to the kitchen to open the door for Tiger, the elderly spaniel, and Smarty, the crotchety old cat, and then put on a kettle to make early morning tea.

The Rectory was a short distance from the village, midway between Dartmeet and Two Bridges, a solid house, capable of standing up to bad weather, its rooms comfortably furnished, the kitchen old-fashioned without modern fitments but with an Aga and a solid dresser laden with plates and china, rather haphazardly arranged. Eugenie moved to and fro at her familiar tasks, roused her parents and laid the table for breakfast. It was still early but her father couldn't be hurried and there were several small chores to be done before they could leave.

Her mother came downstairs first, a woman as tall as her daughter and still with the echo of youthful beauty in her face.

'You go and feed the chickens! She took the bowl of eggs from Eugenie's hand with a smile, and then added, 'Your Father's a bit edgy—you will drive carefully, darling?'

Eugenie opened the garden door. 'Yes, Mother dear, and we'll be back for tea.'

She lingered at the bottom of the garden after she had fed the chickens. Tiger and Smarty, anxious for their breakfast, wove themselves around her as she stood looking about her. The village was out of sight, round the curve of a steep hill, and the only other house in sight was a shepherd's cottage half a mile away. 'Very different from London,' said Eugenie to Tiger, 'and I wonder if I shall ever go back there? Not that I want to but I dare say I shall eventually.'

They had been good to her at the hospital and allowed her to leave on the understanding that she would return as soon as she could and work out the month's notice she hadn't been able to give. It all depended on what the doctors said when they examined her father later on that day.

The drive to Exeter was uneventful. The road was a B class and by no means busy; heavy traffic going to Plymouth and beyond used the fast road further south, skirting the moor, and there were few villages on their route. She had to slow down at Moretonhampstead, a small bustling market town, but after that it was an easy run into Exeter and the hospital.

She took her father straight to the cardiac unit, handed him over to the nurse there, and went to sit in the waiting-room and leaf through the out-of-date magazines there. Rather out of touch for the last few weeks, Eugenie, who loved clothes, found them entirely satisfactory.

Her father was tired by the time the examination was finished and she drove to a quiet restaurant and persuaded him to eat a light meal. The specialist had been pleased with him—another few weeks and he would be allowed to resume some of his lighter duties around the parish, something he was anxious to do after months of convalescence. He talked about it while they ate. 'Another month, my dear, and you will be able to return to your hospital. Do you suppose that you will get back your ward?'

Eugenie speared spring cabbage on to her fork and popped it into her mouth. 'Probably not, Father, but I would be quite glad of a change.'

Which wasn't quite true. She had forborne to tell her parents that once she had done her month's work she would have to leave. After all, the hospital had allowed her to take extended leave—more than two months already—and by now her post would have been filled. When she went back she would work out her month wherever she was needed and then leave. Time enough to tell them when that happened.

She drove home presently, thankful that the day was still fine although there was a bank of cloud in the west climbing slowly across the sky. It was still early in the year and the weather wasn't to be trusted...

Her mother was waiting for them with the tea-table laid and a cheerful fire in the sitting-room, and presently Eugenie went along to the kitchen to cook supper. While she peeled potatoes and sliced vegetables she reflected upon her future. She was twenty-five and heart-whole. She had had more than her share of proposals, both honourable and dishonourable, but although she wasn't exactly sure what kind of man she would like to marry she was quite sure that she hadn't met him yet. Until then she would need to earn her living, this time at a hospital a good deal nearer home. She had talked to the specialist and he had warned her that her father might possibly have a second heart attack, in which case the Reverend Mr Watts would have to return. She did hope not; a nice enough man, she supposed, but with all the wrong ideas when it came to running her father's far-flung parishes. Besides, he had made it plain that he had taken a fancy to her and, from his point of view at least, what could be more convenient than that he should marry the daughter of his rector and, in due course, take over the parish?

'I'll do nothing of the sort,' she told the animals, as they waited patiently for their suppers.

It was raining when she got up the next morning, and the wind had got up during the night, sending low clouds racing across the sky. She listened to a cheerful voice on the radio telling her that there was bad weather from the Atlantic on the way. She went outside and sloshed around in her wellies, feeding the chickens and making sure that the various shed doors were securely fastened and the washing line was empty, and when she got back it was to be told by her mother that the Reverend Mr Watts had phoned to say that he had a heavy cold and could Eugenie possibly do some of his visits for him? There were several, and she decided to take the car and go to the more distant parishioners first—outlying farms and an old man who lived by himself in a tiny cottage isolated from his nearest neighbours. There was a rough track leading to it and she decided to go there first, driving the Land Rover, and since the Reverend Mr Watts was vague as to the old man's circumstances she took a supply of milk and bread and various groceries which he might need. She took the local weekly paper too; if she remembered aright, he liked a good read.

Old Mr Bamber was quite well and delighted to see her. He was fine, he assured her, and looking forward to the warmer weather when he could get out more.

Eugenie offloaded the groceries and the newspaper, washed up the accumulation of dirty dishes in the sink, made them both coffee and sat down for a chat. He knew everyone in the village, so she passed on all the small gossip, promised to give the postman some new batteries for his radio and went on her way.

The farms were off the narrow moorland road but easier to reach; she drank more coffee, enquired after the children, listened patiently to lambing problems, admired new puppies and a litter of kittens, looked at knitting and took a handful of letters to post. It was lunchtime by the time she got home and it was still raining although the wind had died down.

The weather was no better the next day. It was the Mothers' Union in the afternoon and, since the Reverend Mr Watts was still feeling poorly, Eugenie went along to the small village hall, the centre of community activities, and made tea and handed round cake in a practised manner, saying the right things, admiring the babies and small children, lis-

tening to the small problems. I would, she reflected, make a good parson's wife.

The next morning the moors were shrouded in
thick mist, a hazard to any stranger to them but to
Eugenie, who had been born and brought up there,
merely an inconvenience. True, she wouldn't be
foolish enough to go too far from the village, but
what to a traveller might seem a thick blanket with
an occasional glimpse of bleak landscape was to
her quite familiar. She had so often been on the
moors and caught in a sudden mist but all one had
to do, she had pointed out to her anxious mother,
was to stay still and wait for a glimpse of the surroundings—she knew every stone and tree and bush
for miles around and had no fear of the profound
silence the mist brought with it.

By the afternoon the drizzle had ceased but the
mist was as thick as ever. It was almost teatime
when the Reverend Mr Watts phoned. He had a
small house on the other side of the village, perched
off the narrow road on the steep side of the open
moor, no distance away but awkward to reach,
some way away from the first of the village cottages.

Eugenie, listening to his anxious voice, felt sorry
for him. His cold was worse, he complained—if
only he had some cough lozenges or even a lemon,
and he had finished his aspirins.

'I'll come over with whatever you need,' said
Eugenie, cutting short his unhappy complaining.

'You'll never reach me in this mist.'

'Oh, pooh,' said Eugenie, 'expect me in twenty
minutes or so.'

She collected aspirins, a couple of lemons, throat
lozenges and a small bottle of whisky from the

cupboard where, from long experience, her mother stored them, got into her parka and wellies and went out into the darkening afternoon, urged to return as soon as she could. 'I know you can find your way,' said her mother. 'All the same, take care.'

Eugenie found her way unerringly to the village, where the lights from the house windows shone dimly, but once past them she began the climb up the road, keeping well to the bank, hoping that the Reverend Mr Watts would have the sense to switch on all the lights in his house. She began the climb up the narrow path away from the road and saw that he had.

She didn't like him overmuch, but she felt sorry for him, miserable with cold, obviously hating the house and the moor and everything else making life difficult.

'I don't know how you stick it,' he told her. 'If I had known what it would be like when I was sent here—nothing but mist and wind and rain...'

Eugenie had put on the kettle and was squeezing lemons into a jug. 'Oh, come now, you know how lovely it is here on a fine day—the peace and quiet and the gorgeous views and no traffic worth mentioning.'

She made a pot of tea and put an egg on to boil, offered him aspirins and turned up the Calor gas fire. 'You feel rotten, so everything's horrible. You'll be better in the morning. Now sit down and eat your tea and go to bed early and take two more aspirins.'

A practical girl as well as a beautiful one, she had set the table, filled a hot water bottle, taken it up to his bed and come down again to inspect the

larder. 'There's plenty of food here, and as soon
as the weather clears Mrs Pollard will be up to see
to you. I'll ring you in the morning to find out how
you are.'

'You don't need to go? Can't you stay for a
while?'

'My dear man, have you looked outside? It'll be
dark in no time at all and getting around isn't all
that easy.'

'You've lived here all your life. Surely you must
know your way around?'

'Just so. That's why I'm going now. Don't forget
to take this aspirin.'

Making her difficult way back to the road, she
reflected that he hadn't thanked her.

'Men,' said Eugenie, and slithered to a halt as
she reached the road and bumped into a very large
motor car.

Its door was open and an amused voice said, 'An
angel from heaven. You are not hurt?'

A very large arm had steadied her and a moment
later its owner was beside her. He had taken his
arm away but she had the impression that he
towered over her even though she could not see him
at all clearly.

She said, 'No, I'm not hurt. You're lost?'

'Yes. I was steeling myself to spending a long
night in the car. Now I'm hopeful of rescue. Unless
you are lost also?'

'No, no, I live here. Well, not far away. The
village is close by. Where do you want to go to?'

'Babeny...'

'Tom Riley's place. You'll never get there until
this mist lifts. You had better come with me. Mother

will put you up for the night and you can phone him from our house.'

'Your house?' he asked. 'But perhaps there is a hotel or a pub?'

'A pub, but no beds. The nearest inn is miles away at Hexworthy and you've passed that—I doubt if you even saw it.' She added in a motherly voice, 'You know, you really·shouldn't drive around Dartmoor in this weather unless you know your way around.'

'No, no, very foolish of me. Could you get into the car from this side?'

She wriggled her splendid person past the driver's seat without more ado. Only when she was settled did she say, 'Is it a Rolls or a Bentley?'

'A Bentley.' He had got in beside her and she turned to look at him under the car's light. A very large man, bare-headed—his fair hair could be silver, it was hard to see. She could see though that he was good-looking with a high-bridged nose, a thin firm mouth and a strong chin. She wished she could see the colour of his eyes. He was wearing the kind of casual tweeds which, while well cut, looked suitably worn too. Well, she reflected, that stood to reason, didn't it, if he drove a Bentley?

He said nothing, only smiled a little and then said, 'I must rely on you, Miss ... ?'

'Eugenie Spencer. My father's the team rector.'

He offered a large cool hand. 'Aderik Rijnma ter Salis.'

She shook the hand. 'Not English—Swedish? Norwegian? Dutch?'

'Dutch.'

He sounded amused again and she said quickly,
'The road goes downhill for a hundred yards or so
and then levels out as you reach the village. Look
out for the sheep. There's a steep bank on your
right. Keep as close as you can to it—you can just
make it out...'

They began their cautious journey and he asked,
'You walked to wherever you came from?'

'I've lived here all my life. The Reverend Mr
Watts, who's taken over the parish until my father
is well, phoned for lemons and things. He's got a
bad cold.'

'Lemons—and you came out in this weather to
bring lemons?'

'And aspirins. He's from Birmingham and hasn't
got adjusted to the way we live here.'

'That I can well understand.'

'The road curves to the right. Will you open the
window, please?'

When he did she stuck her head out into the mist
for a moment. 'There's a tree stump right on the
corner. Here it is, go a bit to the right—straighten
out now, here's the village.'

The lights were shining dimly through the cottage
windows and the neon light from the village post
office welcomed them, but they were quickly back
in the gloom. 'Not far now,' encouraged Eugenie.
'I must say you drive very well.'

Her companion thanked her meekly.

Her mother had the door open before the car
stopped in front of the house.

'Eugenie, is that you? However did you get
a car...?'

Eugenie had got out of the car, surprised to find her companion waiting for her as she did so, shutting the door for her too. Nice manners, she thought, and plucked at his sleeve. 'Let's get inside. The car will be safe here.' She raised her voice. 'It's me,' she called ungrammatically. 'I've got someone with me; he got lost.'

'Come in.' Mrs Spencer peered towards them. 'You poor man, you must be tired and hungry.'

She held out a welcoming hand as the pair of them reached the door.

'I'm Eugenie's mother.' She beamed up at him. 'You're more than welcome to stay until the mist lifts. The weather forecast is-gales from the west, so there's a good chance it will be clearing by morning.'

They were in the hall and Eugenie took off her parka and kicked off her wellies. 'We waited for you to have tea, so come along in and meet my husband.'

'You're very kind. May I get my bag from the car first?'

'Of course—bring in anything you may need for the night. We have more than enough beds in the house and you can borrow anything...'

He went away and Mrs Spencer took the opportunity to say, 'What an enormous man—wherever did you find him, darling?'

'Just below the Reverend Mr Watts's house. Which room shall I put him in, Mother?'

'The corner bedroom at the back, I think. He's not English, is he?'

'Dutch. Going to Babeny.'

He came back as she spoke. 'You'll want to phone,' said Mrs Spencer. 'It's in my husband's study.' She opened a door. 'Do come into the sitting-room when you're ready.'

There was time to tell Mr Spencer about him before he joined them to be introduced to the rector. Eugenie perceived that the two men were going to get on well together; a chance remark of her father's about the Bronze Age, still strongly evident on the moor, received a reply from their visitor which demonstrated not only a knowledge of that but a lively interest as well. Tea, taken round the fire, was a leisurely meal while the Reverend Mr Spencer expounded his theories about the stone huts, the tors and the very long history of the moors.

It was nice to see her father showing such interest, reflected Eugenie, getting supper ready in the kitchen. Over that meal, presently, the talk turned to just about every subject under the sun. It was only as she was getting ready for bed that she realised that their guest had told them almost nothing about himself. He came from Holland, he was a doctor, he had told them, but more than that they knew nothing. Did he live in England now? Was he on holiday? Why was he going to Babeny? Did he work at one of the hospitals in London perhaps? And just before she dropped off to sleep she wondered, was he married?

By morning the mist had thinned sufficiently for careful driving to be safe enough. Their visitor, eating a hearty breakfast, reiterated his thanks and declared his intention of leaving as soon as possible.

'Well, don't take any short cuts,' said Eugenie matter-of-factly. 'There's a lot of boggy ground.'

He assured her that he would be careful.

Her father didn't come down to breakfast and presently their visitor went upstairs to say his goodbyes, collect his bag and go out to the car. He stowed it in the boot and came back to where Eugenie and her mother were standing at the door.

'I am in your debt,' he told Mrs Spencer, 'and I can never thank you enough for your kindness.' He shook her hand and turned to Eugenie.

'Goodbye—you were an angel just when I needed one—a sensible angel. I am greatly in your debt.'

She offered a hand. 'I'm glad I could help. And do take care.' She wanted very much to know where he was going after Babeny but he had offered no information, not even the smallest hint... She went out to the car with him and waved as he drove away. Extraordinary, she thought, watching the big car disappear round the bend in the lane, to meet a man and know that you loved him even though you might never see him again for the rest of your life. She hadn't supposed falling in love was like that.

She went back to her mother and took her arm. 'I should like to marry him,' she said, and then added, 'Don't laugh.'

Her mother turned to look at her. 'No, dear. Just remember this: if you're meant to meet again and love each other and marry then nothing will prevent that happening.'

Eugenie kissed her mother's cheek. 'I'm not surprised Father married you.' She paused, 'I mean it, Mother.'

'I know you do, darling. Now come indoors and we'll get started on the chores.'

As they washed up together Eugenie said suddenly, 'I don't know the first thing about him and yet I feel as though I know him—have known him all my life.'

She went for a long walk that afternoon and allowed common sense to take over from a daydream which held no vestige of reality. The only thing that was real was the fact that she had fallen in love with a man she was most unlikely to see again. 'Oh, well,' said Eugenie, making her brisk way home again, 'better to have loved and lost than never to have loved at all.'

The temptation to find out about him from Tom Riley was very great but she had no reason to phone that gentleman. He and her father were acquaintances but that was all; besides, it seemed a bit sneaky to go behind Dr Rijnma ter Salis's back . . .

There was a message for her when she got back home. Could she go and see the Reverend Mr Watts about the Mothers' Union and the pram service and could she at the same time bring him some more aspirin?

'He seems rather poorly,' observed her mother. 'You might take him some of the soup I made— there's more than enough for us.' She looked at her daughter's faraway expression. 'Have your tea first, darling.'

The Reverend Mr Watts opened the door to her. He looked woebegone and said peevishly, 'Mrs Pollard hasn't come near me. Just left the milk and papers and called through the letterbox that she wouldn't be coming until I was better. She's afraid of catching my cold.'

'You can hardly blame her,' said Eugenie bracingly. 'She's got five small children.' She went past him into the kitchen to put down the soup. 'You can look after yourself for a day or two, can't you? Would you like the doctor to come? Dr Shaw at Holne is very good. Perhaps you need an antibiotic.'

'No, no, there's no need of that.' He gave her an arch glance. 'Of course, if I had a wife to look after me...'

She ignored the glance. 'Mother has sent you some soup. Now if you will tell me what you want me to do about the pram service and the Mothers' Union. Choir practice as usual, I suppose, on Thursday evening? Will you be well enough to take the Sunday service?'

'I shall do my best. How is Mr Spencer?'

'The doctors are very pleased with him—another month and he will be able to take over at least some of the parish work.'

The Reverend Mr Watts sneezed, blew his nose, and said, 'How splendid. Then my services will no longer be required.' He paused. 'Unless, of course, I might be allowed to hope—Eugenie, would you consider marrying me? We could remain here—in a better house, of course, and I could take over from your father. I must say, with some truth, that I would prefer a living in one of the cities but I can see a good many improvements which need to be made. Living here, in the back of beyond, I suppose one doesn't move with the times as one would in more modern surroundings.'

She was a kind-hearted girl; she also had a fine temper when roused. She allowed her kind heart to damp down the temper and answered him mildly.

'Thank you for your proposal, but I'm sure that I could not make you happy, and I think that you will be much happier if and when you return to a city parish where your enthusiasm will be appreciated. You see, here life is rather different—more basic, if you see what I mean. We live close to nature and nature doesn't change, does it?'

She held out a hand. 'You've been such a help during these last few weeks. We are so very grateful. It must have been hard for you...'

The Reverend Mr Watts blew his nose again and looked pleased with himself despite his cold. 'I believe that I have given your father's parishioners an insight into various aspects of the church.'

'Oh, indeed you have.' She forbore to tell him what they had thought of them. He had, after all, done his best—would still do it once he had got rid of his cold.

She said briskly. 'Well, I must go—there's supper to get and odd jobs around the place.'

He went to the door with her. 'You are happy here?'

'Yes. This is my home...'

'You had no difficulty in getting back yesterday? That awful fog.'

'No difficulty at all...'

'I thought I heard a car just after you left.'

'Sound carries in the mist,' she told him. 'Let us know if you need any help.'

When she got home her mother asked, 'What kept you, love? You've been ages?'

'I have had a proposal of marriage which I refused, and the Reverend Mr Watts told me something of his views about updating us.'

'You were polite, I hope, dear. Oh, I'm sure you were but you do have a hot temper when you are taken unawares. The poor man.'

'He'll go back to his big city and marry someone who'll put his feet in a mustard bath and agree with everything he says.'

She caught her mother's eye. 'I don't mean to be unkind, Mother, he's a very good man, I'm sure, but somehow I can't take him seriously.' She added, 'I don't think he minded too much—me refusing him—I dare say he thought it would be a chance for him to take over from Father later on, even though his heart isn't in rural living.'

'Well, your father is doing so well that he should be able to return to wherever it is he wants to go before very long.' Mrs Spencer began to slice bread. 'I wonder if that nice man found his way safely to Tom Riley's place?'

It seemed that he had, for the next morning the postman delivered a large box addressed to Mrs Spencer. There were roses inside, not just a handful but a couple of dozen, with a note signed A.R. ter S. The note itself was written in such a scrawl that Mrs Spencer wondered if he had written it in Dutch by mistake. Eugenie, invited to decipher it, being used to the handwriting of the medical profession, said, 'No, it's English, Mother. "With grateful thanks for your kind hospitality".'

'How clever you are, love. How very beautiful they are, and so many...'

The fine weather held although there was a chill in the air. Eugenie wrote to offer a tentative return date to go back to the hospital and began to make plans for her future. Regrettably, she was told, her post as ward sister had been filled; she would spend her outstanding month in the operating theatres since the second sister there would be going on holiday. She would be given an excellent reference and without a doubt she would find a similar position to suit her.

She put the letter in her pocket and didn't tell her parents of its contents, only that she would be going back to theatre work instead of her ward.

'That will make a nice change, dear,' observed her mother, whose ideas of hospitals were vague, 'as long as it isn't like that nasty *Casualty* we see on television.'

Eugenie left home during the first week of May, on a cloudless morning when the moor had never looked more beautiful, driving her own little car and hating to leave. She took the Buckfastleigh road since she wanted to stop in Holne to say goodbye to a friend of hers who helped out in the little coffee shop there during the summer months, and although it was still early in the morning the two of them spent half an hour pleasantly enough over coffee. Eugenie got up reluctantly presently. 'I'd better go. I don't want to get caught up in the early evening traffic in London.'

She promised to let her friend know if she got another job, and went back to the car. There was no one much about. The caretaker was still in the little school getting ready for the morning's classes, and the pub on the corner showed no sign of life. In another month, she thought, it would be bustling with tourists, for it was on the very fringe of the moor.

She drove past the reservoir, going slowly because of the sheep, resisting an urge to get out and take one last look around her from one of the tors on either side of the road. Instead she drove on steadily through the narrow streets of Buckfastleigh and on to the A38 which would take her to Exeter and the road to London.

London looked its best in the afternoon sunshine but nothing could disguise the overbearing gloom of the hospital. She parked her car behind the building and presented herself at the porter's lodge to be much cheered by the pleasure of Mullins, the head porter, at seeing her again.

'Nice to see you back, Sister. You are to report at five o'clock.' He glanced at the clock behind him. 'Time enough for you to go to the nurses' home and get the key to your room.'

The warden was new and looked grumpy, and the room to which she led Eugenie was at the back of the building overlooking chimney-pots and brick walls.

'I understand you are leaving at the end of the month and your old room is occupied.'

She went away, and Eugenie reflected that the last warden would have offered her a cup of tea and stayed for a gossip. There was time to make a cup of tea for herself, though, so she went along to the pantry and found two of her friends there. They at least were pleased to see her and, much

cheered by their gossip and several cups of tea, she
made her way to the office.

She was welcomed with as much warmth by the
principal nursing officer as that lady was capable
of showing. An austere woman, handsome and cold
in manner, in her presence Eugenie always felt too
large and too full of life.

She was to start in Theatre in the morning. The
sister she would replace would work with her for
two days until she felt confident. 'That should
present no difficulty, Sister Spencer; you were Staff
Nurse in Theatre and Acting Sister before you had
your recent post, and you have from time to time
returned there for holiday duties, have you not?'

Eugenie agreed politely. She regretted giving up
her ward but she liked Theatre.

She spent the evening unpacking and catching
up on the hospital news, telephoning her mother
and then going to drink tea with those of her friends
who were there, and finally going to her bed to sleep
soundly until morning. She thought briefly and
lovingly of Aderik Rijnma ter Salis before she slept,
and her first thoughts were of him when she woke.
He was the first person she saw as she went through
the theatre block's swing doors.

# CHAPTER TWO

EUGENIE'S beautiful face glowed with delight. She looked up into his calm face. 'I knew we would—meet again, you know. Didn't you?'

He had shown no surprise at the sight of her, and now he said, 'Yes, I knew.' He stared down at her from his great height. 'You are to work here as one of the theatre sisters?'

She nodded. 'For a month. I thought you were a doctor...'

'A surgeon.'

She nodded again. 'Of course—Tom Riley had a pace-maker fitted—you were going to see him...'

'Yes.'

She beamed at him, 'I expect I shall see you again.'

He stood aside to let her pass. 'Oh, undoubtedly.' She thought that she had seen pleasure on his face when they had met, now he was coolly aloof—almost austere. Feeling deflated, she went along to Sister's office and reported for duty.

That lady greeted her with relief. 'Well, at least I'm to have some help,' she grumbled, 'and you do know your way around, don't you? There have been several changes since you were last here—last year, wasn't it? While Sister Thorpe was off sick. I haven't changed, of course.'

Nothing would change Sister Cross. Elderly, bony and hawk-nosed, with small black eyes which missed nothing, she was a by-word among the student nurses who poked fun at her behind her back but were frankly in awe of her when they were sent to work in Theatre. She was remorseless in her insistence on high standards and ruled the three theatres with a firm hand. Even some of the housemen thought twice before displeasing her. But the surgeons loved her for she was utterly dependable.

Eugenie liked her too; they had always got on well once they had each other's measure and she found that Eugenie wasn't in the least scared of her sharp tongue and, when called upon, could work almost as well.

She was bidden to sit down while Sister Cross gave her a brief resumé of the week's work ahead. 'We have a visiting consultant—Mr Rijnma ter Salis—Dutch—a first-class surgeon, specialises in cardiac cases. Over here at Mr Pepper's invitation to demonstrate a new technique with valve replacements. Here for a couple of weeks then goes to Edinburgh and Birmingham. Very civil and easy to work for.'

Eugenie debated to herself whether she should tell Sister Cross that she had already met him, and decided that she had better do so.

Sister Cross heard her out, said, 'Hm,' and told her to go and check the second theatre where a staff nurse would be getting ready for a succession of minor ops.

There was a heavy list, starting with a heart valve bypass 'And you might as well scrub,' said Sister Cross. 'The quicker you get back into the routine the better.'

So Eugenie scrubbed and took the case for Mr Rijnma ter Salis, who treated her with an aloof politeness which she found deflating to her feelings. She hadn't expected him to be overwhelmingly friendly, but on the other hand he had no need to hold her at arm's length with that icy courtesy...

She need not have worried about being thrown in at the deep end. He was unhurried and un-worried as he worked, his massive person bent over the small boy on the operating table, patiently cutting and stitching, so calm that Eugenie, who had been doubtful as to her capabilities, settled down without a single pang of doubt about them. In fact, after the first few minutes, she began to enjoy herself—she had always liked theatre work and it was reassuring to find that she hadn't for-gotten any of her old skills.

The operation wasn't straightforward, taking more time than expected, so that the list, scheduled to finish sometime after midday, was running late. Mr Rijnma ter Salis finished at last, thanked Eugenie politely, stripped off his gloves, stood while the nurse stretched up to untie the strings of his gown, and went away, then Mr Pepper took over for pacemakers and a cardiac catheterisation. She went away to a very late dinner and the afternoon was taken up by an appendicectomy and a strangu-lated hernia. By six o'clock she was more than ready to go off duty, hardly cheered by the reminder from Sister Cross that she would be on call for the night. 'Shortage of staff and holidays,' said that lady. 'The night staff nurse for Theatre is capable of taking any routine case; you will only be called for some-thing she might not be able to manage.'

Eugenie spent the evening writing home, gossiping with her friends, and wondering where Mr Rijnma ter Salis had gone. She went to bed presently feeling vaguely ill done by, although when she thought about it she had no reason to be.

At two o'clock in the morning she was shaken awake by an urgent hand. 'There's a gunshot wound, Sister, pellets in the heart. Can you be in Theatre in ten minutes? Staff's getting ready.'

The student nurse had switched on the bedside light and put a mug of tea beside it. 'You're wide awake?'

Eugenie got out of bed. 'I will be by the time I get to Theatre. Thanks for the tea, Nurse.'

She dressed within minutes, bundling her abundant hair into an untidy and ruthlessly pinned knot and cramming her cap on top of it. She swallowed the tea, turned out the light and went quietly through the nurses' home and into the hospital. It was very quiet, the time of night when most of the patients were sleeping. Only the faint metallic sounds of bedpans being fetched, cups and saucers being arranged in the kitchens and the tread of quiet feet could be identified. She reached the theatre wing and went through the swing doors to be met by the night staff nurse, looking relieved. 'He's here already,' she said. 'I've put everything I could think of out, Sister.'

'Good. The patient isn't up yet?'

'No. Will you scrub now, Sister?'

'Yes. Have IC been warned?'

'Yes, Sister. Will you be able to manage, just the two of us? Night Sister says she is short-handed . . .'

'Then we'll manage.' She smiled reassuringly and went down the corridor to scrub. As she passed Sister's office she was halted.

'Sister Spencer, a moment please.'

Mr Rijnma ter Salis was sitting at the desk, already in his theatre smock and trousers. He looked up as she went in. 'Sorry to get you out of bed. A lad in a street fight, took the full blast from a shotgun in the chest. There are pellets in his heart—a wonder he's still alive—I'll do a median sternotomy. There are a couple of pellets embedded in the pericardium and at least one in the right ventricle. Mr Symes, the senior registrar, will be here in a moment and a couple of the housemen. I understand your technician has been sent for. Do you need more nurses?'

'Night Sister left a message for me to say she's short-handed. Staff Nurse is very competent. If the anaesthetist needs a nurse I'll ask for one.'

For answer he drew the phone towards him. 'Run along,' he told her, 'and get scrubbed.'

He appeared not to see the indignant look she cast at him. She ran along all the same. There was no time to speak her mind to him, but later . . . Run along, indeed! She emptied her head of resentment and went to scrub.

In Theatre presently, sorting out her instruments, making sure that the elaborate equipment was ready with Keith, the technician, she discovered that there was a nurse for the anaesthetist and a senior student to help the staff nurse.

Mr Rijnma ter Salis must have been turning on the charm. Even at two o'clock in the morning she had to admit that he had any amount of that; besides, she was in love with him. She stopped thinking about him then and got on with the business in hand.

Time ceased to matter; she concentrated wholly on her work, aware that Mr Rijnma ter Salis was operating with complete confidence, deftly removing shot from the man's heart and chest wall without any appearance of urgency. It was six o'clock by the time he was completely satisfied that the last foreign body had been removed and began his meticulous stitching up.

That the man was still alive was a miracle, but he was young and had a strong body. It would be touch and go for a few days but his chances of recovery were good. He was borne away to IC, followed by the surgeons and the anaesthetist, and Eugenie and her crew began the task of clearing up. The day staff were coming on duty by the time they were finished.

'You had better go to bed as soon as you've had your breakfast,' said Sister Cross. 'Come on duty at five o'clock and stay until Night Staff Nurse comes on duty.'

Eugenie went off to the canteen, ate her breakfast, although she wasn't awake enough to know what she was eating, and took herself off to a hot bath and bed. Tired though she was, she spared a thought for Mr Rijnma ter Salis. She hadn't seen him once he had left the theatre with a polite word of thanks to her. It was unlikely that she would see him when she went on duty later. She hoped that he wasn't too tired.

One of her off-duty friends called her with a cup of tea just after four o'clock. She turned over in bed and closed her eyes again. 'I'm too tired to go on duty,' she muttered, and buried her head in her pillow.

'No, you're not. There's nothing in, and nothing to do in Theatre but sit in the office and drink tea and catch up on the day's news.'

So at five o'clock, whey-faced from tiredness still but none the less as beautiful as ever, she presented herself at Sister's desk.

'Had a good sleep?' asked that lady. 'Everything's seen to here. There's nothing in Cas for the moment. Nurse Timms will be back from tea in five minutes. She can turn out the dental cabinet. I've left the off-duty for you to sort out, and you can fill in the day book and see to the laundry.' Sister Cross handed over the keys. 'You had better go to bed early.'

Eugenie, who would have gone to bed at that very moment given the chance, said, 'Yes, Sister,' in a deceptively meek voice.

Nurse Timms was a small, meek girl with a prim expression, good at her work but not liked overmuch by her colleagues. She made tea for Eugenie when she got back and then went away to start on the dental cabinet. Eugenie was sure she would do a perfect job on it.

She drank her tea and turned her attention to the off-duty book. There were a number of slips of paper inside it with requests from the theatre staff for particular days off duty. No wonder Sister Cross had left it to her, thought Eugenie crossly. If all the requests were to be granted it would be chaos. Sister Cross had pencilled in a few observations of her own, putting herself down for a weekend and Eugenie for two days in the middle of the week.

'I shall go home,' said Eugenie in a satisfied voice.

'A splendid idea,' said Mr Rijnma ter Salis, coming into the office. He leaned over the desk, reading the off-duty book upside down. 'Wednesday and Thursday—what could be better? I'm going down to Exeter, I'll give you a lift.'

Eugenie had gone pink, and she didn't speak for a moment for she seemed to have lost her voice. Besides, her heart had jumped into her throat and was getting terribly in the way, but since he was waiting for her to reply she took a deep breath. 'That's very kind of you to offer, sir, but I'll drive myself. I have to come back.'

'So do I. Late Thursday evening suit you? You don't have to be locked up at ten o'clock, do you? Presumably only the young are considered in need of a watchful eye?'

Eugenie choked. She said peevishly, 'We older women are trusted to behave ourselves.' She glared at him. Bad temper, did she but know it, gave her good looks an added sparkle.

'No need to get cross. You're tired, of course. But it was worth it; he's doing very well, holding his own. I've just been in to have a look at him.'

'I'm so glad. I do hope all goes well with him.'

Mr Rijnma ter Salis smiled at her and her heart lurched against her ribs.

'You are good at your job,' he observed. 'Your talents are varied—finding your way through thick mist, looking after parsons with heavy colds, and handing instruments at exactly the right time. I'll

be outside at seven o'clock on Tuesday evening—
can't make it earlier. With luck you'll be home
around midnight.'

'I haven't said . . .' began Eugenie. His eyes, very
bright blue, were fixed on her face. 'Thank you,
that would be nice.'

He nodded then, wished her good evening and
went away as quietly as he had come.

There was nothing to hinder her thinking about
him; she polished off the off-duty list in between
bouts of daydreaming. Was he married, she wondered, or engaged? In love with some girl in
Holland? For her own peace of mind she would
have to find out. Perhaps she would be able to discover that on their way to her home.

Tuesday evening took a long time in coming. With
Sister Cross away at the weekend, Eugenie was in
charge of the theatre and although she was kept
fairly busy she was by no means overworked; the
junior theatre sister dealt with minor cases in the
second theatre and there were several part-time staff
nurses, and although there was a list on Monday
Mr Pepper took it. It was annoying to say the least
of it to go off duty when Sister Cross arrived back
at midday, and to find on her return that Mr Rijnma
ter Salis had operated on a bypass that afternoon.

There was no sign of him on Tuesday; she went
off duty at five o'clock uncertain if he had remembered that he was driving her home—and supposing a serious cardiac case needed operating upon?

She changed, picked up her overnight bag and at seven went down to the forecourt, convinced that he wouldn't be there.

He was leaning up against the porter's lodge, very large and elegant and apparently deep in thought. Long before she had reached him he came towards her.

'Hello——' his smile was friendly '—how delightfully punctual you are.'

He took her bag and opened the door and they went outside together. It would be nice, thought Eugenie, if she could think of something to say—light-hearted or witty; instead she remarked upon the weather.

'It looks as though it might rain.'

His mouth twitched. 'I think it very likely,' he agreed gravely as he stowed her into the car and put her bag on the back seat, got in beside her and drove off. No time was to be lost in casual small talk, she supposed, over her initial shyness. She sat quietly as he drove through the city and its suburbs, but once free of the traffic she took the bit between her teeth.

'Are you married?' she wanted to know.

If he were surprised at her question he concealed it very well. 'No.'

'But I expect you're engaged?' she persisted. She hadn't really expected him to say, 'Yes I am,' in a voice which dared her to ask any more questions.

It was a blow and she didn't know why she had assumed that he was heart-whole. He was, after all, what polite society would call eligible—handsome, esteemed in his profession, possessed apparently of enough money to make life very comfortable. She wondered who the girl was, and Eugenie, being Eugenie, proceeded to find out despite the coolness of his manner.

'I expect she's Dutch?'

'Yes.'

'And pretty... Is she—that is, what does she do?'

He didn't answer at once. 'She has a great many friends, travels a good deal and does some social work...'

'But not a job?'

'No. She has no need to work.'

'Well,' said Eugenie, 'that will be nice when you marry. I mean she'll be able to stay at home and look after the children.' The very idea made her feel sick.

'Er, yes, I suppose so.' His words were expressionless. 'Did you phone your mother to say that you would be arriving late in the evening?'

All right, snub me! thought Eugenie, aching with the kind of unhappiness she hadn't known existed. 'Yes, I telephoned her. And if you don't want to talk about your fiancée, that's OK by me.'

His voice was bland. 'Did I say I wished to talk about her? It was you——'

'All right,' she snapped. 'I was only making conversation.'

He laughed then but didn't answer her, and they drove down the A303 for what seemed like a very long time until he pulled in at a Happy Eater.

'I think we have time for a cup of coffee and a sandwich.'

'I'd rather have tea,' said Eugenie haughtily, and skipped away to the ladies. She powdered her cross face, combed her hair and went to find him in the crowded restaurant. He got up as she reached their table. He had the unselfconscious good manners of a man who had been brought up by a good nanny.

'Buttered toast? I'm sure you could eat a slice. We're making good time but we still have a fair way to go.'

She sat down and poured her tea and drank it while a gentle flow of small talk flowed over her, nothing that needed her full attention and requiring nothing more than a brief reply from time to time. It was soothing and her ill-humour melted away; she found herself telling him about her father's illness and the Reverend Mr Watts and how she missed the moor. They went back to the car presently, and although they had little to say to each other the silence was friendly now.

It was late evening by now and dark, and presently it began to drizzle with rain. There was nothing to see and the road ran ahead of them, almost empty of traffic. Uninteresting, even boring, but Eugenie was content; it had been a terrible blow to discover that he was going to marry but just for the moment he was here beside her, large and apparently enjoying her company. As far as she was concerned their journey could go on for ever.

The Bentley tore along, away from the A303 and on to the M5 with Exeter's city lights shining in the distance, and then presently they were on the Plymouth road and, all too soon for her, turning off through Ashburton, climbing slowly towards Poundsgate and then down the hill to Dartmeet. They were travelling slowly now because of the sheep roaming free, but it wasn't long before he took the narrow lane leading to the village and drew up silently outside the Rectory door.

Eugenie glanced at her watch. Just over four hours. They had gone too quickly. He got out and opened her door and she said, 'You'll come in and have something? Mother's sure to have——'

He cut her short. 'I would have liked that, but I must get back to Exeter. I'll see you on Thursday, about six o'clock.'

She was aware that her mother was standing at the door watching them. 'Thank you for the lift,' she told him. 'I'll be ready for you. And do drive carefully.'

He smiled down at her but she didn't see his face clearly in the dark. He got into the car and drove away then, leaving her to go indoors and explain to her mother that he wasn't able to stop.

Her mother led the way to the kitchen. 'Just as long as he has a bed for the night and a good supper to put inside him. He's going to drive you back, darling?'

'Yes, I'm to be ready at six o'clock. How's Father?'

'Very well, considering. Mr Watts has got over his cold and I helped him with the Mothers' Union and Sunday school.' She smiled at her daughter. 'We miss you, love.'

She put a bowl of soup before Eugenie and cut some bread. 'He'll be hungry, that nice Dutchman of yours.'

'He's not mine,' said Eugenie bleakly. 'He's engaged to a girl in Holland.'

Mrs Spencer eyed her daughter. 'But not married. Did you talk about her?'

Eugenie shook her head. 'He didn't want to, I think. He just said yes and no, if you see what I mean.'

'I wonder why. Most men when they're in love with a girl never stop talking about her.'

Eugenie supped her soup and took a huge bite of bread. 'I think he thought I was being inquisitive.'

'And were you, dear?'

'I wanted to know, Mother, and now I do I can do something about it, can't I? Forget him.'

She spoke cheerfully, not believing a word of what she was saying.

Her two days at home were crammed full of odd jobs. Tiger had to be taken to the vet in Buckfastleigh to have his injections, and while she waited for him she did the weekly shopping for her mother and visited old Mrs Ash who lived with her son on an outlying farm. She took a cake with her and a bunch of flowers, for the old lady was celebrating her ninetieth birthday in a week's time, and when she got back home the Reverend Mr Watts was with her father, intent on changing the times of the church services. Eugenie plunged unasked into the discussions.

'Those times haven't been altered in decades. You only want to do so because it's more convenient for you.' She took no notice of her father's, 'Hush, Eugenie,' but went on with some heat, 'What is the point? You'll be gone in another week or two and everything will be changed back again.'

The Reverend Mr Watts, torn between annoyance at not getting his own way and the feelings he cherished towards her, became incoherent, so that she said briskly, 'You see what I mean; I'm glad you agree.'

She gave him a brilliant smile and clinched the matter by saying that she would walk with him back to his house.

When she came back to the Rectory her father said mildly, 'You were rather hard on the poor man, my dear.'

'Oh, pooh, Father. You know you didn't agree with a word he said only you're too nice to say so.' She kissed the bald patch on his head and went away to help her mother get the supper.

It was still raining the next day but there was plenty to do in the garden. She spent the morning pottering happily, digging the ground ready for planting later on—asters and dahlias and chrysanthemums—useful flowers for the church as well as the house. Since it cleared as if by magic while they were having lunch, and there was a steady wind blowing, she washed the kitchen curtains, hung them out and ironed them and hung them up again before changing into the tweed jacket and skirt she had come down in, packing her overnight bag and going downstairs to wait for Mr Rijnma ter Salis.

The last of the rain had long gone and the early evening was clear even if chilly. He arrived punctually, greeted Eugenie with a detached friendliness which ruffled her feelings, accepted coffee and biscuits from Mrs Spencer, chatted briefly to Mr Spencer and observed that perhaps they should be on their way.

He shook hands and Mrs Spencer gave him a warm invitation to call and see them any time he might be travelling in their part of the world. 'We are a bit isolated,' she pointed out, 'but now you know that we are here . . .'

He thanked her with a smile and moved a little out of the way so that Eugenie could say her goodbyes. It was as they were going out of the door that her mother said in a regretful voice, 'Joshua will be so sorry to have missed you, Eugenie. Shall I give him your love?'

She smiled at Mr Rijnma ter Salis. 'The Reverend Mr Watts—he has been helping out while Ben has been ill.'

Eugenie turned a fulminating eye on her parent. 'Don't bother, Mother dear,' she said sweetly, 'he knows how I feel about him.'

In the car presently Mr Rijnma ter Salis asked, 'This reverend gentleman—Joshua? He is understandably smitten with your charms? And do you return his regard?'

'Don't be ridiculous,' snapped Eugenie, 'you know quite well that I don't. He can't even boil an egg . . .'

'You consider that boiling eggs is desirable in a husband?'

'You're making fun of me. But since you ask, I do think that a man should be able to do a bit of basic cooking. Can you cook?'

They were rushing towards Exeter, the city's lights ahead of them.

'I can certainly boil an egg, make toast and fry bacon. I make a good cup of tea, too.'

'Oh, who taught you?' She was being rude and not caring about it.

'My mother. She has always suffered from the illusion that I might marry someone who had none of the culinary arts.'

She might as well go on being rude, she reflected. 'Your fiancée—can she cook?'

'I think it is most unlikely, but since I employ an excellent housekeeper that is hardly a matter which need cause unease.'

'You're rich,' stated Eugenie, aware that she was behaving unforgivably. He would never offer her a lift again...

'Er—you are refreshingly forthright, Eugenie. I'll set your mind at rest by saying that I make a living.'

'You work hard for it, though. I expect you're worth every penny...'

He said placidly, 'I aim to give value for money.'

She fell silent then, and presently he asked, 'And you, Eugenie—from what I have seen of your work, you give value for money too. What do you intend to do when you leave?'

'I'm not sure. You see, I don't want to be tied because of Father. I expect I'll have to go to an agency so that if I need to go home I'll be able to do so. I don't think I shall like it very much, but hospitals want contracts.'

He said mildly, 'You could marry the Reverend Mr Watts—he would, I feel sure, be very satisfied and you would be on hand should your father need you.'

She said forcefully, 'Have you any idea what Joshua is like? Father has had the parish for years, ever since I can remember; it would break his heart if there were any changes. I do not wish to marry the Reverend Mr Watts...'

'That is his loss. You are just right for a parson's wife, bossy and outspoken and managing and capable.'

Her bosom swelled with rage and regret and sorrow that that was how he thought of her. She said quietly, 'This is a pointless conversation, isn't it? Let's talk about the weather.'

He laughed then but remained silent except for the odd remark from time to time—the kind of remark he might have made to a chance passenger he didn't know or someone to whom he was giving a lift as a favour.

At the hospital he got out of the car and helped her out, got her bag and walked with her to the entrance. Here she stopped.

'Thank you for the lift. It was most kind of you.'

He smiled down at her. 'I shall see you again,' he told her. 'Goodnight.'

Of course he would see her again. She was on duty in the morning, wasn't she? And there was a bypass scheduled. 'In the morning,' she reminded him. 'Goodnight.'

She didn't sleep well, her mind too active with thoughts of Mr Rijnma ter Salis, so that she was glad to get up and go to her breakfast and then to Theatre. Sister Cross greeted her in her usual snappy manner, but Eugenie, happy at the prospect of seeing him within the next hour, wished her a cheerful good morning and went to make sure that everything was ready for the morning's work.

She was about to scrub when the senior registrar strolled into the theatre. 'Look out for old Pepper,' he warned her kindly, 'he's a bit snappy this morning...'

'Mr Pepper? Is he doing the bypass?'

'Yes. Rijnma has gone to Edinburgh—a heart transplant—there's an unexpected donor. He'll be there for a couple of days, I should imagine.'

'But he was in the hospital last night...'

He gave her a quick glance. A discreet man who liked her, he had seen the pair of them when they had returned but he wasn't going to say so.

'He drove up overnight. There was no time to be lost—it was suggested that a plane should be chartered but he preferred to drive himself. With a car like his, it wouldn't take any longer than flying up by the time he had got to the airport and been collected at the other end!'

'I hope the op will be successful...'

'It won't be any fault of his if it isn't. He's a good chap.'

He went away and she started to scrub, and presently bore with Mr Pepper's ill humour. She quite liked him but this morning he was living up to his name.

Without Mr Rijnma ter Salis's vast person to distract her thoughts, Eugenie put her mind to her future. She took herself off to a number of agencies and put her name down on their lists for private nurses. There was quite a demand for them but most of them were in London or the Home Counties. Perhaps she would do better to try an agency nearer home—Exeter or Bristol or Plymouth. Mr Symes, doing his best to be helpful, suggested that she tried a private hospital, but they, when she enquired, wanted contracts too. It seemed that opportunities for experienced surgical ward sisters and theatre sisters were few and far between—private nursing, she was told, was more a matter of staying in the patient's own home and performing any nursing duties the doctor might order.

Mr Rijnma ter Salis came back four days later, performed a complicated open heart operation which took hours, thanked her briefly and disappeared again. She had days off again the next day and spent them going round the agencies; time was running out.

Back on duty she met him on her way to dinner. She would have passed him with a polite, 'Good morning, sir', but he put out an arm and stopped her.

'Not so fast. Where have you been?'

'Days off.'

'You leave soon?'

'In about ten days' time.'

'You have another job?'

'Not yet.' She inched away from him. 'I'm rather late for my dinner, sir.'

He took no notice. 'I shall be going back to Holland in two weeks' time. My theatre sister there is leaving to have a baby. I should like you to take over while she is away.'

She goggled at him. 'Me? Holland?'

'Not the end of the earth, Eugenie. A temporary post only but it will give you time to decide what you want to do.'

She opened her mouth to refuse, but he said testily, 'No, I don't want your answer now. Go and eat your dinner and think about it. Let me know in a couple of days' time.'

He had gone, leaving her standing in the middle of the corridor wondering if she had dreamt the whole conversation. Over her shepherd's pie and carrots she decided that it hadn't been a dream; he wasn't a man to waste his time on elaborate jokes or light-hearted suggestions.

'You look very strange, Eugenie,' observed one of her friends at the table. 'Miles away.'

Which she was—mentally at least—in Holland.

# CHAPTER THREE

IT WASN'T difficult for Eugenie to decide what to do about Mr Rijnma ter Salis's offer. It was a gift from heaven, a good omen, although she wasn't sure what good it would do her, except allow her to be with him for a few weeks, when she had been steeling herself to wish him goodbye, never to set eyes on him again. Perhaps she would be able to discover something of his life, find out about his family and his home and this girl he intended to marry.

The knowledge would do her no good, of course, but it would stop her daydreaming...

The tiresome man had gone again; Sister Cross told her that over their coffee the next morning. 'Birmingham,' she said. 'A stab wound—missed the aorta by a whisker—but nicked the pericardium. He went up overnight.'

Wishing to know more, Eugenie said in a diffident voice, 'He seems to work very hard.'

'Too hard. Time he settled down with a wife to nag him. He plans to marry in Holland, so I hear. A good thing too; half the nurses are in love with him.'

To which remark Eugenie had nothing to say. She didn't mind the nurses; it was the girl in Holland, the one who had stolen his heart before Eugenie had met him.

She went away presently to check the theatre, and it wasn't until much later that day that she had the leisure to think about him once more. She could see that taking the job he had offered her could lead to other things; she wasn't a conceited girl but she couldn't help knowing that she was strikingly beautiful, tolerably intelligent and had never lacked eager young men anxious to take her out. She felt fairly sure that given the opportunity she could stir up in Mr Rijnma ter Salis something more than the cool friendliness she had been shown by him. She was nice as well as beautiful, and if he loved this girl then she would be no more than his temporary theatre sister and show the same cool friendliness that he showed her. It would be hard, but she was quite prepared to do it. She told herself that she would make the most of the few weeks she would be with him and then get on with life without him. A bit like a heroine in a romantic novel.

There was still no sign of him; she drove herself home on her next days off and told her mother about Mr Rijnma ter Salis's offer.

'You will accept it?'

'Yes. It will be for a few weeks at the outside. His own theatre sister is having a baby and there's another nurse to replace her, but she isn't available for a time, so I'll fill the gap. It'll give me time to look around...'

Mrs Spencer agreed placidly. It crossed her mind that if Eugenie were in Holland, looking around for another post in England might present some difficulties, but she didn't say so. She remembered uneasily that Eugenie had said that she would like to marry him, and her daughter was a determined young woman.

'I know what you're thinking,' said Eugenie matter-of-factly, 'but you need not worry. I shall enjoy working for him, he is a splendid surgeon, we work well together and he likes me in an aloof way.' She sighed. 'I think that he is a man who would be completely faithful to be the girl he loves.'

'Yes, dear, he will make a fine husband. She's a lucky girl.'

Her mother glanced at her daughter's resolutely cheerful face. 'Now tell me more about this new job. A splendid opportunity to see something of Holland.'

'I haven't the faintest idea where I'm to go—he just asked me if I'd work for him for a few weeks and told me to think it over. I haven't seen him since and I've not been told when he's coming back.' She added vaguely, 'He comes and goes...'

'I dare say he'll be at the hospital when you get back, love.' She added, 'Joshua Watts is coming to supper. Your father needs to discuss something with him.'

Eugenie said crossly, 'Oh, Mother...!' and added quickly, 'Sorry, of course he has to come. Only he will *look* at me.'

'Yes, dear, I know what you mean. But if you go away for a few weeks he'll probably be gone by the time you come home.'

'That's true. I'll be very nice to him.'

Which was a mistake, since he took it as an encouraging sign and assumed an air of possession which infuriated her. Saying goodbye after supper, she took care to impress upon him that she was

going away for some time and he would probably
be gone by the time she came home again.

He smiled and patted her hand, giving her an
arch look which made her feel quite sick. 'I may
still be here,' he told her, adding, 'Your father isn't
too strong.'

Rage choked her. She took her hand away and
shut the door firmly upon him before going to the
kitchen to help her mother with the dishes.

'He's been tiresome?' asked Mrs Spencer.

'Tiresome—tiresome? Mother dear, he's awful—
smug, thick-skinned and conceited. He won't have
to stay much longer, will he?'

'No, dear, your father feels that he'll be able to
manage with the rest of the team to back him up.
By the time you are home again he will be gone.'

'You will be all right if I go? I had intended to
get a job with an agency so that I could come home
if you needed me.'

'I'm sure that Mr Rijnma ter Salis will allow you
to come home at once if we need you, Eugenie, but
your father is so much better and Dr Shaw will keep
an eye on him.'

So Eugenie went back to the hospital more or
less satisfied that life for her parents was almost
back to normal and she could get on with her own
life again. Something she would do when she returned from Holland.

She was having coffee with Sister Cross while the
junior sister took minor surgery in the third theatre
when he walked in, accepted coffee, passed the time
of day with Sister Cross and asked abruptly, 'Have
you decided to accept my offer, Eugenie?'

She was very conscious of Sister Cross's surprised look. 'Yes, thank you, sir, I should like to work for you.'

'What's all this?' demanded Sister Cross. 'It's the first I've heard of it.'

Mr Rijnma ter Salis gave her one of his charming smiles. 'Eugenie is most kindly going to work for me for a few weeks until my present theatre sister's replacement is able to take over.'

'And where is this? In Holland?'

'For the most part. I like to have my own theatre sister working with me—there's no need here, of course, but it makes things much easier in the Middle East or America or some of the Mediterranean countries.'

Sister Cross, after due thought, agreed. Eugenie said nothing; life had suddenly become full of exciting possibilities.

She was roused from these pleasant thoughts by Mr Rijnma ter Salis's businesslike tones. 'I believe you leave at the end of next week, Sister. I shall be returning within the next few days but I will see that arrangements are made for your journey. You have a passport?'

She nodded.

'Good. I'll let you have the details before I leave.'

He went away presently and Sister Cross observed that she was a lucky young woman. 'Good experience for you, Sister Spencer, and probably he will give you an excellent recommendation—you mentioned that you were considering agency work—they will snap you up—the private hospitals always have several openings. He will be a great help for your future.'

Indeed he would. It was a great pity that she had no wish for a career, only to be a wife—his wife.

There was a list in the afternoon and, Sister Cross being off duty, Eugenie scrubbed for it. The last patient was being wheeled away as Sister Cross came back on duty and Eugenie got back into her uniform and sat down to fill in the book before handing over. Sister Cross was in the mood for a gossip so that it was some time before Eugenie was free to go.

She pushed the theatre suite doors open and found Mr Rijnma ter Salis on the other side.

His 'You're late,' uttered in a testy voice, annoyed her. She was tired and unsettled and vaguely unhappy and she answered him with a snap.

'I'm tired...'

'In that case I won't keep you. I'm going to Liverpool this evening and may not see you before I go back to Holland. If you had been in a better mood I had considered taking you out for a meal so that we could discuss the job. But since you don't feel up to it I'll see that you get written instructions and all the information you may need.'

'Oh, I didn't mean——' began Eugenie, and was cut short by his impassive,

'Think nothing of it. I'll see you in Groningen.'

He stood aside to let her pass and, since a quick look at his face told her that remonstrating with him wouldn't do any good at all, she murmured a goodnight and went past him. Really the man was tiresome! she reflected, expecting her to fall in with his plans without argument. She frowned. She wasn't absolutely certain where Groningen was, for a start. How was she to get there and when?

She need not have worried. The next morning when she went on duty she found a large envelope addressed to her on Sister Cross's desk. She hadn't a chance to open it before that lady came on duty herself and cut short any idea which Eugenie might have had about disappearing into the nurses' cloakroom and reading its contents.

'You'd better scrub,' she told Eugenie. 'There's a lot of paperwork I must see to. A thoracotomy, isn't it? I hear Mr Pepper is in a bad temper.'

As indeed he was.

It wasn't until she went off duty that evening that Eugenie had the opportunity to open the envelope. Its contents were considerable. There was a plane ticket, a typed timetable and instructions, and a brief note signed, 'Rijnma ter Salis' in a scrawling hand. She read the note first. She was asked to read the instructions carefully, keep a minute account of her expenses on the journey as they would be refunded to her, remember to bring her passport and be prepared to travel on the day indicated. Three days after she left the hospital, nice time in which to gather together clothes and make sure that her mother and father were all right.

She read further. Her flight was a direct one to Groningen. Since she would be on call for possible emergencies on certain days, it would be necessary for her to live at the hospital. She would have two free days a week, three hours off duty each day and would be given a week's notice to leave. This was unusual, it was pointed out, but the exact date upon which the theatre sister was to take up the post permanently had not yet been determined. She would receive the same salary as her Dutch counterpart, paid monthly. The particulars of the hospital were concise and detailed and after she had read them through she couldn't think of a single question she needed to ask.

Very efficient, she thought, and added in a mutter, 'But he might have told me himself.' Which unfair remark, overheard by one of her companions in the sitting-room of the nurses' home, was questioned. There was no point in being secretive; she explained where she was going when she left and was greeted with cries of envy, demands to know the details and the general opinion that she had certainly fallen on her feet.

Of course she had, she reflected, lying awake in her bed later. It was a breathing space in which she could decide what she wanted to do next, be more certain that her father had made a good recovery and, above all, she would be with Mr Rijnma ter Salis. She thought about him for several sleepy minutes and slept on the thought that she must discover his Christian name as soon as possible. He had mentioned it when they first met, but she couldn't remember it. At a pinch, she would ask him next time they met.

There was no likelihood of that now since he wasn't even in the country. She contented herself with replenishing her wardrobe and reading as many guidebooks on the Netherlands as she could lay her hands on.

Packing the last of her things, going round wishing her friends goodbye, Eugenie supposed that she should feel some regret at leaving the hospital; after all, she had trained there and stayed on to become a well-liked and skilled member of the nursing staff. Perhaps if there had not been Mr Rijnma ter Salis she would have minded more than she did. As it was she got into her car, waved goodbye to those of her friends there to see her off, and drove herself home. It was still early morning and a fine day and, once she had left London behind, she began to enjoy herself. She had two more days before she left for Holland, and Dartmoor in May could be a delight.

Two days weren't enough, of course; her clothes had to be unpacked and those she was taking with her repacked—blouses and skirts and thin sweaters and, taking the advice of one of the guidebooks, a raincoat and a short showerproof jacket and, since there was always a chance of warm weather, a jersey dress and a washed silk dress in a pleasing shade of honey. Only at her mother's insistence did she cram in a chiffon pleated skirt, chocolate-brown, with its accompanying top of coffee-coloured crêpe.

'It is a good thing,' observed her mother, watching her tucking away undies, 'that you wear almost nothing underneath, for those wisps take up no space at all.' She looked out of the window at the sunlit garden. 'Of course, if it gets really warm you could buy some dresses there.'

Eugenie nodded absently. 'I wonder what the uniform is like,' she mused. 'I should hate not to wear a cap...'

'Well, dear, I dare say you will be in your theatre kit most of the time. You will phone as soon as you get there, won't you?'

'The moment I can, Mother and I'll write as often as possible. If I'm busy I'll send postcards.'

Eugenie closed her case and locked it. 'There, that's done, now I can enjoy myself. Does Father want me to do anything for him while I'm at home?'

They went downstairs together and found her father in his study.

'I shall preach on Sunday,' he told them. 'Joshua will take the service.'

'When is he leaving?' Eugenie wanted to know.

'In a month's time, I believe. He is to have a brief holiday before going to a parish in Liverpool.'

'You'll be all right without him?'

'Oh, yes, my dear.' Her father's voice was dry. 'Joshua's coming to supper this evening.' His eyes twinkled behind his old-fashioned spectacles.

It was her mother who added, 'He invited himself, darling—he wanted to say goodbye to you.'

Eugenie choked back words which would have shocked her parents.

'I thought he'd done that once. I suppose I can't have a headache?'

'Darling, you never have headaches and he might come round tomorrow to see if you're better.'

'I could go to bed early because I'm tired...'

The Reverend Mr Watts arrived early and stayed late and, since she could see that her father was tired, Eugenie stayed late as well, listening politely to his earnest remarks about the parish he was going to, how he would run it and what he intended doing—he had it all planned and she had to admire him for his enthusiasm, although her admiration was rather soured when he stared straight at her and observed that he had hopes of a supportive wife, someone, he added, who understood church work and its attendant responsibilities.

'I'm sure you'll find someone,' said Eugenie briskly, and was equally brisk when he at last went home, ignoring the length of time for which he held her hand and his murmured 'If ever you should change your mind, Eugenie.'

'Why is it,' she asked her mother, drinking a cup of tea in the kitchen after her father was safely in bed, 'that the wrong people like you?'

Which wasn't exactly what she meant, although her mother understood her well enough.

The one day left to her was a happy one, pottering in the garden, saying goodbye to friends in the village, taking Tiger for a walk. 'I shall miss this,' she told him, leaning against a tor and absorbing the view. She knew it by heart but she wanted to make quite sure that she would be able to recall it while she was away.

Matt from the village stores was going to drive her car back for her; he sat beside her as she left the next day, very early in the morning, and if he hadn't been there she might have wept a little. As it was, she waved gaily to her mother and father standing in the porch, and drove down the lane to join the road which would take her to Ashburton and the fast road to Exeter and beyond.

She had known Matt all her life; he was a churchwarden, the local taxi if one was required, and the sub-postmaster. He also ran the stores, selling just about everything anyone living miles from the nearest town might need. He said now, 'It's a treat your father's taking over again. We'll take good care of him, Eugenie, and your mother too.'

'I know you will, Matt, I wouldn't go otherwise. And don't forget, if there's anything—if anything goes wrong, phone me. I've put the phone number in the glove box. I'll come back at once.'

'They'll let you? You're working for that doctor chap, aren't you? He sounded a good sort.'

'He is. Besides, he owes me—remember, I found him when he was lost in the fog...' They both laughed.

'Nasty things, those fogs, if you don't know your whereabouts,' said Matt.

At Heathrow she bade him goodbye with real regret. 'I'll send you a card,' she promised, kissed his cheek and went to check her luggage in.

The flight was uneventful. She ate her snack lunch, quite hungry by now since it was two o'clock, read the in-flight magazine, checked her handbag and looked out of the window although there was nothing to see since they were above the cloud. It was restful staring at nothing, but she was roused from that by the stewardess offering boiled sweets, and presently they were told that they were about to land.

The land below the clouds looked green, with here and there a village but no large towns. There was no one in the seat next to her, but as the stewardess checked her seatbelt, she asked, 'Is the airport a long way from Groningen?'

'Ten kilometres to the centre of the city. You are to be met?'

'I think so.' The girl smiled and went away and Eugenie stared out of the window, watching the ground get nearer and nearer. There had been nothing about being met in her instructions. Presumably there was some kind of bus or train to take her into Groningen, and Mr Rijnma ter Salis had taken it for granted that she was sensible enough to get herself to the hospital. More likely he had left it to a secretary or someone similar to write out the instructions.

She was one of the last passengers to leave the plane. There was no one to hurry her and she would have to find her own way. She collected her case from the carousel and went through the empty customs shed and out into the reception hall.

She put down her case and looked around her. There were a number of people there but it was by no means crowded, not like Heathrow. She started to read the various signs, rotating slowly, getting her bearings. She came full circle and found Mr Rijnma ter Salis looming over her, her case in his hand.

'Well,' said Eugenie, unable to think of anything else to say.

He smiled in what she considered a patronising manner. 'Eugenie, welcome to Groningen.'

'There is nothing in your instructions to say that I would be met,' she said coldly.

'I thought it would be a nice surprise for you.' He spoke blandly and although she was overjoyed to see him she frowned, for she suspected that he was laughing at her.

'It is certainly a surprise. Am I going straight to the hospital?'

She blushed, for it sounded as if she were expecting to go somewhere with him—tea in a café would have been nice.

'Yes. The car is outside, shall we go?'

She followed him to the entrance and saw the Bentley parked close by, and as they crossed the road she saw that there was someone in it. A woman, sitting in the front seat, her face turned half away. Mr Rijnma ter Salis opened the car door and ushered Eugenie into the back seat, at the same time saying, 'Saphira, let me introduce Eugenie Spencer.' He glanced at Eugenie. 'My fiancée...'

He went to put her case in the boot and Saphira said with casual politeness, 'Hello, you had a good trip...?'

Her smile was perfunctory but her blue eyes made a swift study of Eugenie's person. She was good-looking, with regular features and fair hair cut very short. In her early thirties, thought Eugenie, who had used her own eyes to good effect, and I don't like her. She smiled. 'Very comfortable, thank you.'

Mr Rijnma ter Salis got into his car, then nodded his handsome head to some remark Saphira made in a low voice, looked over his shoulder to ask if Eugenie was comfortable, and drove away from the airport.

Eugenie looked out of the window, taking care to have an interested expression on her face while she allowed her thoughts to bubble and boil. Why had he brought his fiancée to meet her? An unspoken reminder that he was going to marry and had no interest in Eugenie as a woman, only as a theatre sister? At Saphira's request, she didn't doubt. Was he regretting offering her the post?

Worse, had he an inkling of her feelings towards him? She went hot at the thought... Suddenly she wished that she hadn't come, but since she was here she would have to make the best of it; she would give him no cause to complain about her work and would take care to be professional at all times.

'I'm taking you straight to the hospital,' said Mr Rijnma ter Salis over one shoulder as they reached the outskirts of Groningen. 'You'll be glad to settle in.'

Eugenie said thank you in a sedate voice and Saphira said in her high, penetrating voice, 'You're coming back with me, Aderik?'

Her English was almost perfect. It would be, thought Eugenie sourly, but at least she remembered now what his name was. Rather nice too, she decided.

Groningen looked delightful, she decided, as they drove through streets lined with patrician houses, across a wide square and then presently a second one.

'Easy to find your way round,' she was told. 'All the main streets start from them. The hospital's close by.'

A handsome building, reached through a wide archway, probably old, thought Eugenie, peering from the car window, but added to without spoiling its appearance at all. Mr Rijnma ter Salis got out, fetched her case from the boot, handed it to a porter and helped her out.

'Goodbye,' said Saphira, sounding bored. 'I hope you will enjoy working here.'

Eugenie thanked her in the same sedate voice, and he glanced at her with a faintly lifted eyebrow although he said nothing, merely led her through the entrance and handed her over to the head porter who picked up the phone and spoke into it, and then stood leaning against the desk.

'Thank you for meeting me,' began Eugenie, and held out a hand.

'The least I could do,' he murmured. 'I'll introduce you to the *directrice*...'

That lady arrived a moment later, a tall woman with silvery blonde hair and blue eyes. Her expression was severe but she smiled as Eugenie was introduced to her, bade her welcome and turned to Mr Rijnma ter Salis.

'Thank you for meeting Miss Spencer. A familiar face is welcome when one arrives in a strange country.'

They shook hands and he said kindly, 'I'll see you some time tomorrow, Eugenie. I'm sure the *directrice* will tell you anything you need to know.'

He went away then and the two of them, with the porter carrying the case, crossed the entrance hall and went along a wide corridor and into the office. 'You will want to go to your room—have a cup of coffee or tea—but first I will give you a leaflet of information which will give you some idea of the hospital and its routine. You will come and see me in the morning at ten o'clock, Miss Spencer. If you have questions I will answer them then.'

Eugenie collected the papers, and with the porter still at her heels went back the way she had come to the row of lifts at the back of the hall. On the fourth floor they got out and, with the porter leading her now, went through double doors into a small hall with a staircase on one side. The figure who came bustling out of a door to meet them was cosily stout with a round face crowned by white hair upon which rested a severe white cap.

'Zuster Corsma.' Eugenie was given a beaming smile. 'You are most welcome, Miss Spencer. We will go to your room and I will arrange for you to have tea—the English drink tea very often, do they not?'

Eugenie's spirits had been rather dampened by Mr Rijnma ter Salis's welcome and the *directrice*'s coolly pleasant greeting, but now she warmed to the little lady's cheerful pleasure at meeting her. The three of them went up the stairs and along a passage lined with doors. Zuster Corsma opened the last one and ushered Eugenie inside, the porter put her case on the floor and left, and she looked around her.

The room was small but pleasant and nicely furnished, with a window overlooking a wide strip of lawn and beyond that what she supposed was the back of the hospital.

Zuster Corsma patted the bedcover into perfection, twitched the curtains, and said cheerfully, 'It is nice, is it not? There is a bathroom on the other side of the passage and a kitchen at the other end where you may make tea or coffee and sandwiches if you are hungry. Now I will leave you; tea will come presently and when you are ready you will come down to my office.'

She trotted off and Eugenie went to look out of the window again. The hospital was large and, as far as she could see, in the centre of the city, but that was something she would discover later. First she must unpack, read the papers she had been given and go and see Sister Corsma...

She had almost finished unpacking when a young girl brought the tea; Eugenie went to the window again and drank it and then made her way back to Zuster Corsma's office, and from there to a store room where uniforms were found for her. After that she was taken on a tour of the hospital and introduced to a number of nursing staff, whose names she instantly forgot. She ate her supper in a daze. It wasn't too bad when someone addressed her in English but the cheerful voices, chattering away in what seemed to her to be nonsense, made her wonder if she had bitten off more than she could chew. She went to bed finally, convinced that she would never sleep, and went out like a light.

Of course in the morning everything was fine. She sat between two girls who spoke good English, listening to their advice as they ate their breakfast, and when she went on duty she felt immediately at home in Theatre even though when they weren't actually talking to her everyone else spoke Dutch. Mr Rijnma ter Salis wasn't operating until the afternoon and she spent the morning shadowing the theatre sister on duty. The list wasn't long and the surgeons, after meeting her, took her for granted, which was reassuring. She scrubbed for the last case, a simple appendix, just to get her hand in— if it wasn't for the language problem, she might have been back in her own hospital.

The bypass was scheduled for two o'clock, and punctual to the minute Mr Rijnma ter Salis walked into Theatre. He nodded at Eugenie as though he had been accustomed to see her there for years, enquired politely if she was ready and began the operation. There were, of necessity, a number of people there. Eugenie had met them all that morning but now, gowned and masked, she couldn't tell one from the other; only Mr Rijnma ter Salis, bent over his patient, was recognisable to her, asking her for this or that instrument from time to time, murmuring to his two assistants and from time to time saying something in English so that she didn't feel out of it.

Presently the patient was wheeled away to Intensive Care, the men left the theatre and she began to clear with two of the nurses. It was long past teatime; the pleasant habit at her own hospital of going to the office with the surgeons and sharing a pot of tea and a tin of biscuits seemed unknown here. Thank heaven she was off duty at six o'clock, rather late for tea but there was bound to be a café or coffee shop open near the hospital . . .

There was no one around when she finally reached her room. She changed into the jersey dress and the showerproof jacket, sensible shoes because her feet ached, and slung her bag over one shoulder. From her window the weather didn't look too bad, the sky was a cold blue and the sun was rapidly sinking behind the tall city buildings. She pulled a scarf out of a drawer and stuffed it into a pocket. One of the guidebooks had mentioned that it rained a good deal.

She went downstairs in the quiet house. Presumably everyone else was on duty or already out, but as she reached Zuster Corsma's door it opened and Mr Rijnma ter Salis came out.

'Settling in?' he wanted to know. 'No sign of nerves in Theatre this morning or this afternoon.'

'I should hope not,' said Eugenie. She had been taken by surprise—a delightful surprise—but she remembered that she had resolved to behave with professional aloofness and then, since she had perhaps been rather too brisk, she added, 'The theatre is magnificent, sir.'

'Had your tea?' He was standing in front of her, taking up most of the width of the passage.

'I'm off duty. I shall have tea somewhere in the city...'

'I know just the place,' and as she opened her mouth to speak, Zuster Corsma popped her face round the door.

'You go to have tea with Mr Rijnma ter Salis? That is a good idea. You are a little lonely, I think, and there is no one off duty with you.'

Eugenie said rather wildly, 'No, no, Zuster, I'm going to explore before supper.'

'Tea first,' said Mr Rijnma ter Salis, and took her arm with some remark to Zuster Corsma that she was unable to understand.

'I do not wish...' began Eugenie, as she was hurried to the entrance hall and out of the vast doors.

'Tut tut, you're being foolish. You rescued me on Dartmoor; now I am rescuing you in Groningen.' He was walking away from the hospital, still holding her arm. 'There is a place not too far away in Gedempte Zuiderdiep where they serve a very good tea. I sometimes meet Saphira there.'

'It's too late for tea...'

He didn't bother to answer and a few minutes later he pushed open an elegant glass door, sat her down at a small table by the window and settled himself opposite her. People around them appeared to be eating dinner; all the same they were served tea without any fuss. Nice strong tea, little sandwiches and a plate of simply mouthwatering cakes. Eugenie forgot her good resolutions and smiled across at him. 'This is very nice. Saphira wouldn't mind?'

'Mind? Why should she mind? As a matter of fact she suggested it!'

# CHAPTER FOUR

THE delicious forkful of cream and pastry Eugenie had just popped into her mouth turned to ashes. She was being given a treat, was she? And, worse than that, a treat which Mr Rijnma ter Salis hadn't thought of himself. The original dislike of Saphira which she had felt on meeting her became even stronger. She was clever too, demonstrating her hold over him—she might just as well have told Eugenie to keep her hands off him. Perhaps in someone of a less robust nature the hint would have been taken but Eugenie, scenting a challenge, instantly decided to take it up.

She said in just the right kind of voice, 'How very thoughtful of her and how kind.' Her smile was guileless. 'Your fiancée is beautiful, isn't she? I've always wanted fair hair...'

A remark which naturally enough caused him to look at her own glorious dark mop, as it had been meant to do.

'Are you getting married soon?' Eugenie sounded politely interested. 'I'd love to see a Dutch wedding.'

He passed his cup for more tea. 'No definite date,' he told her smoothly. 'I'm sure you will have an opportunity to see a wedding while you are here. Most of them are at the Raadhuis.' He began to tell her a little about the city. 'I'm sorry I'm not free to start you on your exploring. Was there somewhere special you wanted to see?'

'It's too late for the museums and churches. Zuster Corsma told me that it is late-night shopping. I thought I'd have a look before I go back—some of the sisters suggested that we might go out for supper when they come off duty—I'll just have time to take a quick look round.'

She uttered this fib without turning a hair. Let him understand that she was in no need of concern for her amusement; a fib or two would do no harm. 'Thank you for my tea, it was kind of you to spare the time.' She looked out of the plate-glass window. 'The squares are over there, aren't they, to the left? You won't mind if I go now before the shops close?'

He called for the bill at once, agreeing pleasantly that there was still time to look around, looking at her from under his lids with an instantly suppressed smile. He saw her safely across the street, making sure that she was going in the right direction, and then walked back to the hospital, looking thoughtful.

Eugenie, her feelings ruffled, spent some time window-shopping until the thought of supper drove her to look for a place where she might eat. There were any number of cafés and restaurants. She chose one which looked half-empty, first studying the menu outside to make sure that she had enough money with her. It was a self-help place; she took her tray and joined the queue. There was a wide variety of food and she chose what she could recognise easily: croquettes and a salad and a cup of coffee which she took to a small table in a corner. The croquettes were excellent; she finished her supper, drank her coffee and got up to go.

'Alone?' asked a tall man who had been sitting near her. 'You're English, aren't you?'

'Yes, I am.' She went past him and then found him behind her.

He caught up with her when she reached the pavement.

'Don't worry, I do you no harm, but you are far too pretty to be on your own. I will find you a taxi or perhaps a bus.'

She turned to look at him. 'You're very kind, but I'm quite all right. I'm working at the hospital and it's only ten minutes' walk away.'

'So I will walk with you. You are a nurse?'

'Yes, and it is really quite unnecessary...'

'I will come all the same. You do not need to talk to me. I have sisters of my own.'

'Don't they go out alone?'

'Of course, but they are not foreign.'

He had no more to say, but at the hospital entrance wished her a polite good night, reiterated his advice not to go out alone until she knew her way around, and shook her hand. 'I'm very grateful,' said Eugenie.

Mr Rijnma ter Salis, driving past, raised his eyebrows and quenched a strong feeling of annoyance. Eugenie, not seeing him, said a final goodbye and went into the hospital.

They met in Theatre the next morning. Mr Rijnma ter Salis was to perform a mitral valvotomy. He arrived punctually, wished her good morning and set to work without fuss. There were, of necessity, a number of people there; the heart-lung machine needed skilled handling but Eugenie, concentrating on her instrument trolley, remained unfussed. The operation was successful, the patient borne away and the theatre cleared. Mr Rijnma ter Salis, pausing by Eugenie as she stood having her gown untied, addressed her coldly. 'A word with you, Sister, if you please.'

She followed him down the corridor to the office, wondering what she had done wrong. As far as she knew, everything had been just as it should; she hadn't kept him waiting for a second and had been careful to hand him the special instruments he liked to use.

He opened the door and she went past him and sat down at the desk.

It was a small room. He leaned up against a wall, his hands in his pockets. 'You lost no time in finding an escort yesterday evening,' he observed blandly. 'Someone you knew?'

'I'd never seen him before in my life. Why do you ask, sir?'

'I am surprised that you allow yourself to be picked up so easily, Eugenie.'

She sat up very straight. 'That is an unforgivable remark, sir. It is also untrue!' She choked back rising rage. 'I am not in the habit of picking up men.'

'No, no, of course not. I expressed myself very badly. You are a beautiful woman, Eugenie, and I am sure that you are quite safe on Dartmoor, but you are in a foreign country with no knowledge of the language and you are—forgive me for saying so—innocent.'

She tossed her head. 'What utter rubbish,' she said tartly. 'I'm twenty-five years old and even if I'm a rustic born and bred I've lived for years in

London's East End. I can take care of myself.' She
gave a snort of indignation. 'If you think that of
me, I can't think why you offered me this job.'

He said placidly, not in the least put out, 'You
are a sensible girl and an excellent theatre sister,
but Saphira was quite right when she suggested that
I should warn you...'

Eugenie opened her mouth and closed it again
on the thoroughly unsuitable words crowding her
tongue. She tried again. 'Pray tell your Saphira to
mind her own business. I'm sure she means to be
kind and helpful—she is, I imagine, a good deal
older than I am and probably knows more about
being picked up than I do...'

She stopped. Mr Rijnma ter Salis hadn't moved
but she pushed her chair back against the wall. If
she could have gone through it she would have
done; the rage in his face sent cold shivers down
her spine. She had gone too far, she knew that, but
he had goaded her into losing her temper. She made
herself look at him. 'Hadn't you better go before
you hit me?'

She sat for quite a while after he had gone. She
had been horribly rude, she had insulted his
Saphira. He would not forgive her for that,
probably he would send her back to England...

Her Dutch counterpart came on duty presently
and she was free for the afternoon. It was far too
late for her midday meal and anyway she couldn't
have eaten anything. She handed over the keys and
made her way through the hospital. The theatre
block was cut off from the wards by a long corridor with lifts at one end and a staircase at the
other. She wandered to the stairs and started down

them and came face to face with Mr Rijnma ter Salis on the first landing.

'Get a coat,' he told her, 'and meet me at the doors.' He sounded quite pleasant.

She searched his face and he looked steadily back. There was no point in not doing as he asked; he was going to sack her and the sooner it was over the better. She said quietly, 'Very well.' Then she went past him on her way to her room.

It took her five minutes to change into a skirt and sweater and the showerproof jacket, and then another minute or two to reach the entrance. He was waiting for her.

'We will walk to the gardens at the Prinsenhof,' he told her, 'We need to talk.'

It wasn't a long walk and neither of them spoke. Not until they were in the gardens did he say, 'We will find a seat.'

The surroundings were beautiful, somewhere she had intended to visit—two hundred and fifty years old and a delight to the eye. She supposed with a wry smile that if she was to be dismissed this was as good a place as any.

There were seats cunningly placed in the hedges, sheltered and while in full view offering privacy, but when he stopped by one she said quickly, 'If you don't mind, I'd rather walk.' She wouldn't have to look at him then.

There were few people there. Halfway along the path he stopped. 'I owe you an apology. I had no right to speak to you as I did. You must believe that. And I lost my temper . . .'

She gave him a direct look. 'I said some dreadful things about your Saphira. I didn't mean a word of them and I'm sorry. I lost my temper too.' A truthful girl by nature, she hoped she would be forgiven for the lie. Perhaps it wouldn't matter if it made things easier for him. Men, she reflected, were so blind, especially when they were in love. He must be deeply in love with the woman, although she couldn't think why; she was all wrong for him.

She held out a hand. 'Shall we forgive and forget? We get on well in Theatre, don't we? I don't see why we can't be civil to each other when we meet.'

Somehow she had managed to give the impression that, although she was prepared to let bygones be bygones, it didn't matter to her one way or the other. It seemed to have worked; he took her hand. 'That seems to be a sensible way out of our difficulties.' He smiled suddenly. 'Could we bury the hatchet over coffee and sandwiches? Too late for lunch and too early for tea, I'm afraid.'

'That would be nice. This is a very beautiful park...'

They walked on while he told her its history, and presently went into a small café in a side street where they drank delicious coffee and ate *uitsmijters* which, despite the strange name, was ham and eggs on bread. The helpings were large but Eugenie polished hers off with a healthy appetite and agreed readily enough to another pot of coffee. Presently he looked at his watch. 'I have some patients to see at three o'clock—I'll walk you back to the hospital and pick up the car.'

They walked back briskly, to all intents and purposes good friends once more, but beneath her calm friendliness Eugenie was bottling up a strong resentment against Saphira. It was a good thing that she was unlikely to meet her.

They parted at the hospital, Eugenie with the slightly aloof manner of a working colleague who, while friendly, has no wish to enlarge upon that friendship. There was a coarctation of the aorta scheduled for the early afternoon the next day. Eugenie went off duty in the morning since she was to scrub for it. Mr Rijnma ter Salis greeted her civilly as he entered Theatre, exchanged a few remarks with the numerous people present and got to work. It took a little longer than they had expected, for the ends of the aorta would not come together and he was forced to insert a graft, but finally he was satisfied and the patient was wheeled away to Intensive Care while Eugenie and her staff began the task of clearing up. The theatre had to be prepared for the morning and it was almost time for her to go off duty when Mr Rijnma ter Salis came back.

'You had better have a day off tomorrow. We shall be flying to Madeira early in the morning on the day following. A ventricular septal defect—the Dutch consul. Have my instruments ready for me to check, will you? I'll be back later this evening. Take enough clothes with you for ten days, though I hope we'll be back by the end of a week. Summer clothes and uniform, of course.'

Eugenie said with calm, 'Does Sister know?'

'Yes. I shall want you at the door by seven o'clock in the morning the day after tomorrow.' He nodded briefly and went away.

'I have always fancied a visit to Madeira,' said
Eugenie to the empty room, 'even at a moment's
notice.'

She went away then and dealt with the instruments, laying them out neatly so that he could see
at a glance if there was anything else he might want
with him, and by the time she was finished Night
Sister was there to take the keys.

'You'll need some cotton dresses,' she observed,
hearing Eugenie's news.

At least she had a day off in which to see to her
own wardrobe, reflected Eugenie, making lists and
counting the notes in her purse.

She was up early and off to the shops almost as
soon as they were open. A cotton skirt and several
tops, she had decided, and two cotton dresses. She
could travel in the jersey dress and pack the washed
silk. She would need sandals and a swimsuit. Maybe
she wouldn't have the chance to wear it, but surely
she would have off duty. She found what she
wanted: a blue denim skirt, a couple of loose cotton
tops and a striped shirt blouse, a flowered print
dress with short sleeves and a chambray dress in
cream and nutmeg-brown. She added sandals and
a hyacinth-blue swimsuit and went back to the hospital to pack her case. She was passing the café
where Mr Rijnma ter Salis had taken her for tea
when she saw Saphira sitting at a table in the
window with another woman. She glanced at
Eugenie and then waved casually before turning
back to her companion. Eugenie didn't wave back,
and her smile was cool and slightly puzzled as
though she wasn't sure who Saphira was. She went

on her way satisfied that Saphira might possibly be
annoyed because she was not recognised instantly.

In this she was correct. Saphira, telephoning Mr
Rijnma ter Salis that evening, since he had declared
himself far too busy to take her out to dinner, remarked upon it. 'That girl you brought from
England to work for you—I saw her today. I waved
but she smiled as though she had no idea who I
am...'

'Perhaps she hasn't. After all, you only saw each
other for a few moments in the car.' He was only
half listening while he studied the patients' notes
before him.

'Why can't you take me out to dinner? I had your
message when I phoned, but surely you stop work
to eat? Besides, I'm bored.'

'Ah, yes, I was about to ring you. I'm going to
Madeira tomorrow on an early morning flight—I
shall be there for a week at least.'

'Are you taking that girl with you?'

'Eugenie is my theatre sister, Saphira, that is why
she is here. Naturally she will be with me.'

'All that hair,' snapped Saphira, 'and she's going
to be fat in another year or two.'

'Neither of which makes any difference to her
skill in the operating theatre.' His voice was icy.
'You're being childish, Saphira.'

She slammed down the receiver and he went back
to his work. Presently he put down his pen and sat
back in his chair. Eugenie, he reflected, would never
be fat; curved in all the right places, certainly, but
she was a big girl. Her rich brown hair framed a
lovely face. He wondered idly how long it was when
she unwound the neat knot into which it was

pinned. He picked up his pen again; he had a good deal of work to do before they left in the morning.

Eugenie was up early. Dressed and ready, she made tea and toast in the nurses' home and went down to the entrance with her case and a shoulder-bag. Mr Rijnma ter Salis was there, looking so unexcited that she quelled her own excitement, wished him a sober good morning and got into the car. She wondered about their journey, but he had looked at her rather strangely—checking that she was suitably dressed, perhaps?—and she hadn't liked to ask questions. Her curiosity was satisfied presently when he said, 'We're flying to Schiphol and picking up another plane there.' He didn't speak again until they reached the airport. They flew in a charter plane and transferred to another charter plane at Schiphol—no customs, no fuss. Eugenie was impressed. She ventured to ask, once they were airborne, 'Do you always travel like this?'

'No, no. This is laid on by the government—and an emergency.' He opened his case. 'In case you don't know Madeira, I brought along a guidebook for you to read.'

She received it gratefully. The flight would take several hours, she supposed. Madeira was all of fifteen hundred miles from the Netherlands. She opened the book and began to read, glad of something to do since Mr Rijnma ter Salis was frowning over a handful of papers.

Presently they were given coffee and biscuits and, lulled by the sight of the clouds, she dozed off. A ntle tap on her shoulder wakened her.

'We're coming in to land.' Mr Rijnma ter Salis smiled at her. 'You'll see Funchal presently once we're through this cloud.'

A moment later she saw the island beneath them, the town tucked between two great headlands, houses, still far below, climbing up the sides of the mountains behind it. As she looked, the clouds drifted away and the sun shone on to the white houses and sparkled on the sea. She was enchanted.

They were met at the airport by a serious young man driving an imposing car. He welcomed her to the island and then, with a word of apology, lapsed into Dutch as Mr Rijnma ter Salis got in beside him after seeing her into the back of the car. It left her free to look around her as he drove into the town, down a wide curved road and towards the heart of it. Before they reached the centre they passed a park with a casino facing the sea, and the young man swept the car into equally beautiful grounds and stopped before the hospital.

Mr Rijnma ter Salis got out, opened her door and observed, 'I'm going to take a look at our patient—you too, of course, and perhaps while I'm with him you could take a quick look at the theatre. We're putting up at the consulate. I suggest that after lunch there we come back and you can make sure that things are to your liking. The hospital staff are co-operative and friendly.' His eyes searched her face. 'You're not tired?'

'Not in the least,' declared Eugenie, longing for a large pot of tea and somewhere where she could put her feet up.

They went into the hospital with the young man and she was led away by an elderly woman with black hair and eyes and a haughty manner. Which, Eugenie discovered, wasn't haughty at all, just the way she looked. She was taken to the theatre, a good deal smaller than the one at Groningen but well equipped. The heart-lung machine was already in place and she was introduced to the technician who, to her relief, spoke good English. In fact all the nursing staff she met did that, so any qualms she might have had about language difficulties were put at rest and she spent a short time making herself familiar with the place. She had her lovely nose deep in an instrument cupboard when Mr Rijnma ter Salis joined her.

'Satisfied? Good. Now come and meet our patient.'

The man lying in the bed was not yet middle-aged although he looked ill. He was handsome, or would be when he was well again, and despite his condition he smiled at Eugenie and whispered something as she took his hand in hers, speaking Dutch and turning towards Mr Rijnma ter Salis, who laughed and answered briefly.

'What did he say?' she asked as they went out to the car.

'He thinks that you are beautiful.' Mr Rijnma ter Salis's voice was dry and the quick glance he gave her sent the colour into her cheeks.

'I didn't know that women still did that,' he said.

'Did what?'

'Blush.'

She didn't look at him but got into the car and looked out of the window during the short drive to the consulate.

The vice-consul made them welcome and handed her over to the consul's wife, a tall, rather stout lady with a charming smile and bright blue eyes.

Her English was more than adequate and she welcomed her warmly. 'I am so worried,' she said as she ushered Eugenie up the stairs. 'My husband is so very ill but of course you know that. To have Aderik here is a consolation, for he will operate and will make my husband well again.' She paused on the stairs. 'It is very hard when you love someone and he is ill.'

Eugenie murmured soothingly; Mevrouw van Tegge was a woman one could warm to instantly.

Her room was charming, its balcony overlooking a large garden with the sea beyond. 'I've put you at the back of the house, Miss Spencer, it is sometimes noisy at night...'

'Thank you, and would you call me Eugenie? Everyone does.'

'A pretty name. But then you are a very pretty girl. And you must be very good at your job or Aderik would never have wanted you to work for him.'

There wasn't an answer to that; Eugenie smiled and her hostess went away with the remark that lunch was waiting for her as soon as she came downstairs.

Her case was already in the room but there wasn't time to change her dress. She did her face and her hair and went downstairs again to find Mr Rijnma ter Salis standing with Mevrouw van Tegge at the open doors to the garden.

They lunched out of doors and, since the afternoon was well advanced by that time, went

back to the hospital. The operation was to be early
in the morning—half-past seven—and she put
everything ready as far as she could; she would need
plenty of time to make her last-minute adjustments
in the morning and nothing must be left to chance.
Satisfied at last, she went back to the waiting-room
on the ground floor after being shown round the
hospital by a friendly nurse. Presumably Mr Rijnma
ter Salis was still there.

He was; he came presently, the anaesthetist and
two doctors with him. They gazed at her with open
admiration and the younger of them said, 'When
you are free, Miss Spencer, I shall have pleasure in
showing you something of Madeira.'

'I shall like that.' She spoke with rather more
enthusiasm than she felt, but Mr Rijnma ter Salis
was staring hard at her with an amused smile.

There was, she reflected, no hope of him showing
her anything which wasn't to do with tomorrow's
operation.

They went back to the consulate presently and
had a late cup of tea before she went upstairs to
shower and change into one of the cotton dresses.

She would have to be at the hospital by half-past
six at the latest, she was told at dinner, and she
went up to her room as soon as she politely could
after they had had their coffee. She wasn't nervous;
she knew that she would be able to cope, but she
was tired. It had been a long day. A not very satisfactory one either, she told herself, getting into
the bed with its ornate dark wood headboard; Mr
Rijnma ter Salis had been considerate and
thoughtful of her comfort but he had been
very aloof...

*        *        *

It was a beautiful morning as they drove to the hospital along quiet narrow streets. They had nothing much to say to each other; they had eaten their rolls and drunk their coffee without waste of time, and beyond one or two remarks about the morning ahead of them, Mr Rijnma ter Salis had very little to say. They parted company when they reached the hospital and she went at once to the theatre to see to his instruments, check the equipment, the lighting, the positioning of the tables and trolleys and machines. That done to her satisfaction, she had a last-minute talk with the three nurses who were to assist her, and went away to scrub.

She was standing surrounded by her trolleys, very composed, when the patient was wheeled in and, hard on his heels, Mr Rijnma ter Salis with his two assistants.

Time didn't matter after that. At long last he straightened upright, as placid as when he had made his first incision. There had been a tricky moment when he had decided to patch the defect with a plastic patch since sutures wouldn't hold, but that had been successful. He exchanged a few words with the anaesthetist, added his thanks to Eugenie, and left the theatre.

There was a prodigious amount of clearing up to do, but first Eugenie was whisked away by the other nurses to a small room away from the theatre to drink a mug of coffee. They all talked at once— the operation had been a great success and they had all fallen in love with Mr Rijnma ter Salis.

'He's engaged,' Eugenie told them, 'and she's very pretty.' She didn't want to talk about that; in-

stead she asked what she should see while she was
on Madeira.

Despite their protests, she went back to the
theatre to help with the clearing up. Mr Rijnma ter
Salis's instruments had to be cleaned and auto-
claved, his needles and sharps dealt with, the whole
checked and repacked ready for use. It took some
time and, although the others went to a late midday
meal, she chose to stay and finish this exacting task.
She fetched the case the instruments were kept in
and arranged everything neatly inside, shut and
locked it and stood a minute, suddenly tired and
hungry.

Mr Rijnma ter Salis, coming silently into the
theatre, paused to look at her. She had her back to
him and in her green smock and trousers, her cap
pushed back on untidy hair, she presented an un-
glamorous sight.

'If you've finished, we'll go and have a meal.
I'm famished and I imagine you are too?'

She spun round as he spoke. 'Oh, hello—well, I
think I'm supposed to have my lunch here. Thank
you all the same.' She pulled off her cap and a lot
more hair tumbled down. 'Is Mijnheer van Tegge
going to do?'

'I'll say yes, but keep my fingers crossed. It's too
soon to be sure. Now get out of that thing and come
with me.' He smiled suddenly. 'You did well,
Eugenie, thank you. I'll be at the door.'

She got into her denim skirt and a cotton top,
poked her feet into sandals, bundled her hair up in
a rough and ready fashion and sped down to the
entrance. He was there, talking to the two men who
had assisted him, and they stood chatting for a few

minutes before he said, 'I'll be back in a couple of hours.' He took her arm and went out into the street.

It was very warm and the streets were quiet. 'Siesta,' he told her, 'but I know where we can get a good meal.'

He walked her away from the main streets and the sea and turned up a narrow street of small shops and cafés. He stopped at one of these and ushered her in through the open door. It was dim inside with a handful of tables and chairs, half of them occupied.

He sat her down and the waiter came at once. 'A long cool drink?' asked Mr Rijnma ter Salis of Eugenie. 'Would you like to try a maracuja? Passion fruit juice with iced soda water.' When she nodded, he said, 'And I'll have a beer.'

He spoke to the waiter, and said, 'Can you speak Portuguese?'

'No—just a few words, enough to get a meal and ask the way.'

She looked at the menu and wondered what it all meant. If she were on her own she would never dare to eat...

As though he had read her thoughts, he said carelessly, 'The big cafés and restaurants have English menus and the waiters speak some English; you'll be quite all right on your own.'

A gentle hint, she wondered, not to expect much of his company?

'Shall we have *filete de espada*—fish—and a salad?'

It was delicious and they ate it slowly, mulling over the morning's work. The conversation, thought Eugenie, would have inspired no hint of jealousy in his Saphira's breast, could she have overheard it.

She peeped at her companion as they ate their *bolos de mel*, which was, after all, only an elaborate version of Madeira cake, and said on an impulse, 'I expect your Saphira would have liked to come with you.'

He eyed her coldly. 'I do not mix business with pleasure.' His voice was as cold as his eyes. She wished that she had held her tongue.

He had taken her out to lunch though, she reflected, walking back to the consulate after they had parted at the hospital, but there again he must have considered it a business lunch...

She spent the rest of the afternoon with Mevrouw van Tegge, reassuring her as best she could. 'I'm sure you will be allowed to see your husband very soon, but he does need to rest a great deal and don't be upset when you see him; he's on a ventilator and there'll be an ECG monitor. It all looks a bit frightening but they'll be disconnected as soon as possible.' She added for good measure, 'There are some very good nurses there.'

When the phone rang Mevrouw answered it and handed it to Eugenie. 'For you. It's bad news?'

'I want you here, Eugenie. For the evening and possibly the night. Everything's going well, but the senior nurses on duty must have some time off. Bring Mevrouw van Tegge with you. She can visit for a few minutes.'

Eugenie put down the phone. 'You can visit now, Mevrouw. I'm coming with you and staying to relieve the nurses. I'll get into my uniform.'

'We'll have the car.' Mevrouw van Tegge rang the bell and Eugenie flew up to her room to change. Ten minutes later, they were at the hospital.

Mr Rijnma ter Salis met them. 'Your husband is doing splendidly. Don't worry about his looks, just take my word for it. You can have five minutes. He's barely conscious but he'll know you're there.'

He sounded so kind, and yet when he turned to Eugenie his voice was coolly formal. 'Thank you for coming, Eugenie. I'll go over the charts with you before I go. You'll have a nurse with you but she's not experienced.'

The intensive care unit was small but well equipped. Eugenie checked the charts with the two nurses going off duty until Mevrouw van Tegge had been ushered out of the room, and then listened carefully to Mr Rijnma ter Salis's instructions.

'You'll be all right until about six-thirty tomorrow morning?' he wanted to know, and when she nodded he said, 'I'll be in later on and don't hesitate to ring if you want me. Dr Borge is on call; he'll be in and out.'

The nurse who would stay with her might not be experienced but she was quick and sensible and spoke fluent English. The pair of them settled down to a busy night—half-hourly pulse, aspirations, reading the ECG monitor, blood pressure. They moved silently to and fro in their white gowns, heedless of the time. Dr Borge came frequently, and just before two o'clock in the morning Mr Rijnma ter Salis came too, pronounced himself satisfied and went away again.

He was there again at six o'clock, wearing the appearance of a man who had had a good night's sleep and a splendid breakfast, in contrast to Eugenie who was tired to the bone and starving. The snatched cups of coffee and half-eaten sandwiches during the night had by no means satisfied her. She wished him a grumpy good morning and then became very professional, detailing the night's progress meticulously.

'Good. Now go away, Eugenie, and sleep and eat—everything's laid on for you at the consulate. I shall be here all day, but come on duty at ten o'clock tonight, please.' He laid a large hand on her shoulder. 'You are my right hand. Another forty-eight hours and we can relax.'

She was so weary that all she really wanted to do was to put her head on his shoulder and weep. Her brief, 'Very well, sir,' gave no indication of that.

# CHAPTER FIVE

EUGENIE was quite herself by the time she had eaten an enormous breakfast, had a shower and got into bed. It was because she had been tired that she had felt so low-spirited but now, already half asleep, she remembered that Mr Rijnma ter Salis had called her his right hand. Hardly romantic, but satisfying to her sadly deflated ego. Perhaps he would be less standoffish now...

She slept until early evening, got up and showered and went downstairs to find Mevrouw van Tegge in the drawing-room.

'Tea,' said that lady at once, 'and then a little while in the garden for some fresh air before your supper. The car will take you to the hospital so you have time for all this.'

'You are very kind, Mevrouw. Have you visited Mijnheer van Tegge?'

'Indeed, yes. He progresses. Aderik has been with him for the whole day—in and out—you understand. One more day, he tells me, and we are out of the wood.'

Her blue eyes filled with tears. 'I am so happy...' Mevrouw van Tegge wiped her eyes. 'Here is your tea and then we go into the garden. Aderik told me that you were to take the air, that you were strong but that you must remain so for a few more days.'

Not by any stretch of the imagination could she call that a compliment, decided Eugenie silently.

Why could she not have been born small and dainty, with an appealing manner which brought men running to do everything for her?

She had a second cup of tea and reflected that Mr Rijnma ter Salis was obviously of the opinion that, because she was a big girl and sensible with it, he could expect her to work all hours. She disregarded the fact that he worked all hours himself and that, since she had the skills needed in the intensive care unit as well as in theatre work, he would expect to make use of them.

The garden was large and a blaze of colour—bougainvillaea, orchids and dragon flowers, palm trees and vivid blue periwinkles. They strolled around with Mevrouw's Pekinese at their heels before returning indoors to eat the supper waiting for them.

Eugenie, hungry again, enjoyed the tomato and onion soup—a speciality of Madeira, her hostess told her, as was the *espetada*—barbecued beef—and once again the *bolos de mel*. It was a warm light evening; they had their coffee on the terrace overlooking the garden before she got into the consulate car and was driven to the hospital.

She was already in uniform. She got into her gown and went along to the little anteroom adjoining the patient's room. Mr Rijnma ter Salis was writing at the table as she went in. He got to his feet, bade her a friendly good evening and wanted to know if she had slept well.

'Oh, yes,' said Eugenie, 'and eaten like a horse too.' She glanced at him in the lamplight and saw the weariness in his face. 'It must have been a long day...'

'Everything is satisfactory. I shall take him off the ventilator tomorrow if all goes well. All the usual observations, please. I shall be sleeping here again and Dr de Castelo will be on call. We will take a look at the patient now...'

Mijnheer van Tegge's condition had certainly improved. He was still very ill and exhausted but he managed to wink at Eugenie before dozing off again. She listened carefully to Mr Rijnma ter Salis's instructions, bade him a good evening and set about her night's work. She had a different nurse to help her tonight—a small placid girl, quick and sensible, who saw to the minor chores which let Eugenie deal with the observations and half-hourly checks. She wasn't as tired as on the previous night and, although she didn't leave the patient for more than a few minutes at a time, the night went quickly. Dr de Castelo came several times, and around midnight Mr Rijnma ter Salis had come for a final check before he went to bed. He was there again at six o'clock in the morning, ready to read her report and the charts.

'I shall want you here tonight, Eugenie. The last one if he can cope without the ventilator. Then perhaps you would work whatever hours are suggested.' He smiled at her. 'I think that we may be able to leave in four or five days' time.'

Her 'Yes, sir' was a model of correct behaviour towards a consultant surgeon.

She woke earlier that afternoon and took herself out into the town after she had had tea. Mevrouw van Tegge was at the hospital, and she left a message to say that she would be back in an hour or so and then went out of the consulate gates into the street.

The porter at the door had lent her a map and she walked quickly through the main street to the Zarco statue and turned into the broad avenue, past the Governor's Palace, and down towards the sea front. There were a great many people about and all the shops were open. She would have liked to linger at them but that could come on another day when she had more time. She reached the Avenido do Mar and walked a little way along it, getting her bearings. The coastline was spectacular. If she had the chance before they returned home she meant to see more of it. There were any number of buses; she had only to ask...

She returned presently and found Mevrouw van Tegge back from the hospital. Her husband had had a splendid day, she told Eugenie. The ventilator was switched off and he had spoken to her. 'Your dear Aderik,' she exclaimed, 'what a splendid man, how can we ever thank him?'

Eugenie murmured gently, wishing that he really were her dear Aderik.

His businesslike manner towards her when she went on duty presently gave the lie to any such wish. He was pleased, she could see that, but he was cautious too. She received his instructions in silence, merely saying briskly 'Very well, sir' when he told her that he would be sleeping in the hospital for one more night. Dr de Castelo would be on call again, and the nurse who had helped her during the first night.

His, 'Goodnight,' was abrupt but she forgave him; he was tired and the last two days and nights had been dicey.

The night went well; Mijnheer van Tegge was improving steadily now, everything was functioning as it should and he was fighting back. Eugenie handed over in the morning to a nurse flown in from Lisbon, gave her report to Mr Rijnma ter Salis and went off to breakfast and her bed.

He had walked to the hospital entrance with her, discussing the further treatment of his patient, when Dr Borge joined them and, as she made to leave them, asked her if she would care to have dinner with him that evening. 'I could show you something of Funchal,' he told her in his friendly way, 'if you are not too tired. You will be on day duty tomorrow?'

Mr Rijnma ter Salis said levelly, 'I believe it is hoped that Eugenie will come on duty tomorrow afternoon to relieve the new nurse.'

'Well, in that case I'd very much like to have dinner with you.' She smiled at Dr Borge. 'I'm sure that there's a great deal to see.'

She promised to be ready by seven o'clock that evening, bade the two men goodbye and walked to the consulate. Over breakfast she told Mevrouw van Tegge of her invitation.

'Now that will be nice. You are here for so short a time—Aderik tells me that he hopes to return to Holland in two days' time, three at the latest. You must see as much as possible before you go.'

Eugenie slept through the warm day, dressed in one of the patterned dresses when she awoke, did her face and hair nicely and went down to wait for Dr Borge. He was already there, talking to Mevrouw van Tegge, and whisked her away without loss of time.

'A meal first,' he told her, and walked her to the Caravela restaurant close to the sea. It was a popular place and already almost full, but he had booked a table by a window with a splendid view of the sea and harbour.

He was a pleasant companion, she discovered, full of information about the island, delighted to answer her questions. The food was delicious and since she wasn't going on duty until the next day she sampled the Madeira wine, a dry one before they ate—Sercial—and Boal to finish.

It was dark by the time they had eaten but there were still a few shops open and the streets were well lighted. They walked around for a time and he pointed out the main streets, the best shops, the cafés where she could go on her own if she wished.

It had been a delightful evening, she told herself as she got ready for bed much later. Dr Borge was a nice man but she wished that he had been Aderik... She must stop thinking of him as Aderik.

She was taken completely by surprise the next morning when the serious young man who had met them at the airport arrived at the consulate and invited her to have lunch with him.

'Well, I'd love to,' said Eugenie, swallowing surprise, 'but I'm on duty at one o'clock.'

'It is half-past ten,' he told her seriously, with not a vestige of a smile. 'I will show you the cathedral and the public garden on the Avenida Manuel Arriaga and we will have coffee in Reid's Hotel. I will see that you are not late on duty.'

'In that case,' said Eugenie, anxious to see as much as possible of Madeira while she was there, 'I'd love to come.'

'We will walk,' he told her, 'so that you have an opportunity to see as much as possible.'

So she fetched the straw hat she had bought and clapped it on to her dark head and, looking cool and pretty in a cotton dress, set off very willing to be shown the town. There was a great deal to see, but Jan van Daal had no intention of allowing her to waste time lingering in the flower market or peering up the narrow streets leading away from the town up towards the heights behind it. Instead he took her to the cathedral, the Governor's Palace and two of the three museums. The third, he explained, he hoped to be able to show her later. The museums were interesting but she longed to be out in the glorious sunshine, peering into shop windows, buying the useless things tourists bought, stopping at a café to drink lemonade and, when they passed the Madeira Wine Lodge, she longed to go inside to look at the huge wine casks and taste the wine. This, she was told, was a great waste of time. Jan looked at his watch and said prudently that it was time they returned to the consulate. 'You will need lunch before you go to the hospital.'

Then she thanked him prettily for spending the morning with her, and when he suggested a visit to the third museum she said vaguely that she had no idea when she would be free. 'We shall be leaving very soon now.' She smiled at him in her friendly way. 'It was so kind of you to show me something of the town.'

She was nonplussed when he said gravely, 'I considered it to be my duty.'

She saw Mr Rijnma ter Salis only briefly when she went on duty, and the following day, going on duty in the morning, she didn't see him at all until she was leaving in the early afternoon.

He was talking to Dr Borge and, as she passed them with a murmured 'Good afternoon,' he put out an arm and brought her to a halt.

'Ah, just the person we wanted to see,' he told her. 'Our work is done here, Eugenie. I hope to leave the day after tomorrow, all being well. Consider yourself free until then. We will take the afternoon flight out on the following day. That should give you time to browse round the shops.'

She thanked him in a colourless voice, already busy with plans. Certainly she must do some shopping for presents and she would need to return to the hospital to wish everyone goodbye, and over and above that she intended to take a bus—any bus—and see something of the island.

'If you are not too tired,' said Mr Rijnma ter Salis at his most silky, 'we will leave the consulate at eight o'clock. We can go inland and see something of the island and then come back to Funchal. Have you been to the Madeira Wine Lodge and sampled the wines?' And when she shook her head, still thinking up a polite refusal, he said, 'Good, you will enjoy that, won't she, Borge?'

'Indeed you will, Eugenie, and what an opportunity to see the sights with someone who knows his way around. One can miss so much, even with a guidebook.'

He gave her a wide smile. 'It is good that you are to be rewarded for all your hard work here. You have been splendid.'

Mr Rijnma ter Salis patted her in an avuncular manner on her shoulder. 'Eight o'clock,' he reminded her, 'and don't be late. We mustn't miss a moment of our day off, must we?'

Her 'Very well, sir' was uttered in a meek voice, although she would have liked to speak her mind about people who took things for granted without bothering to discover other people's wishes. She went on her way, while peevishness at his high-handed methods and the delight of the prospect of spending a whole day with him battled for supremacy. Delight won, of course.

She spent the afternoon in Mevrouw van Tegge's company, listening to that lady's happy plans for her husband's convalescence, and presently sat down to dinner with her. Of Mr Rijnma ter Salis there was no sign.

Serve him right if I don't go with him, reflected Eugenie as she got ready for bed, knowing that of course she would go. Mevrouw van Tegge had thought it a splendid idea and had ordered early breakfast for her anyway.

It was going to be a warm day; she got into one of the cotton dresses, thrust bare feet into her sandals and, with her hat in her hand and a shoulder-bag with all her money in it, went downstairs. It wasn't quite eight o'clock but he was there, leaning against the Saab he had borrowed from the consulate.

He bade her good morning, stuffed her into the front seat, got in beside her and drove off.

'I should like to know where we are going,' said Eugenie in a starchy voice.

'First to the botanical gardens—there's a marvellous view of the harbour and the town from there—you like gardens?'

'Oh, yes—and they're all so different here.'

'Then we'll press on to Camacha up in the hills—they make the wickerwork there, if you should want a shopping basket?'

She forgot to be starchy. 'I do, and so does Mother...'

The gardens were beautiful, full of exotic flowers and plants. She could have lingered for hours but presently Mr Rijnma ter Salis suggested that they might drive on. 'So that you can see as much as possible,' he pointed out.

Camacha was at the end of a winding road into the hills, a small place where the inhabitants sat working at their baskets and chairs and plant-stands beside the stalls laden with their wares. Eugenie bought two baskets and would have bought a wicker chair if there had been a means of conveying it back.

He took her across the island through the hills above Funchal, stopping at Monte for coffee, and then driving on along the winding road which took them eventually to Camara de Lobos where they had lunch: sardines cooked on an open grill in a small restaurant overlooking the sea. They drove on presently, along the coast road, stopping for tea at Ribeira Brava and strolling round the shops there.

Eugenie was bubbling over with delighted interest and the pleasure of Mr Rijnma ter Salis's company. He was proving to be an ideal companion; not only did he know the island quite well, he answered her questions with patience and waited patiently while she examined the contents of the shops wherever they happened to stop. The embroidery was beautiful; she bought a cloth for her mother, table mats and handkerchiefs, and admired the pottery, but by then her money was running out, allowing her only enough to buy a small dish. He carried her parcels, stowed them in the car and drove on again, telling her snippets of information about the places they passed. He was without a doubt a hundred times more interesting than Jan van Daal. Just for that day, she reflected, she would forget that very shortly they would revert to their professional attitude towards each other; she would forget too his Saphira and the unknown future once she was back in England. She was going to enjoy every moment of it.

Apparently he felt the same way. Driving back towards Funchal in the late afternoon he asked, 'Do you want to go back to the consulate and dress up? We could dine in one of the hotels—Reid's or the Sheraton or would you rather dine in Camara de Lobos? There's a good country restaurant there and we can go as we are.'

'Yes, please.' She added, 'It would spoil the day to have to dress up...'

He glanced at her, smiling. 'We agree about so many things, Eugenie. We'll go to the Café Ribamar and eat. It'll be simple—tomato and onion soup again, I dare say, and some sort of fish and either *bolos de mel* or ice-cream.'

'It sounds lovely and I'm hungry.'

The restaurant was small and crowded but they were given a table by the open window and, sure enough, they were offered tomato and onion soup and several kinds of fish or *espetada*. She chose the soup and the fish and it arrived beautifully cooked and piping hot so that, despite the glass of Sercial she had had while they waited, she agreed to a bottle of Vinho Verde to cool it down. The service was leisurely and friendly; they sat for almost two hours, and afterwards she couldn't remember what they had talked about, only that she had been happy and content.

It was quite late when they went back to the car and began the drive back, talking idly of their day. It was a splendid night with a full moon and thousands of stars. The moonlight shone on the water and save when they passed a village tavern the night was quiet. They could see the town of Funchal ahead of them ablaze with lights and when they reached it, in contrast to the quiet of the country, the town was alive with people.

'Would you like to have a drink somewhere?' he asked her.

'No. No, thank you. It's been a lovely day and thank you for taking me. I've enjoyed every moment.' She sighed gently. 'I'll never forget it.'

He didn't answer, but drove through the crowded streets until he reached the consulate. At the door she said, 'Don't get out—you have to garage the car, don't you? I expect you'll tell me in the morning what time I have to be ready to leave.'

She could have saved her breath. He was opening her door before she had finished speaking and held it while she got out. 'I'll bring your parcels in presently,' he told her, and walked her to the door where the porter sat dozing.

'Good night, sir,' said Eugenie, and offered a hand. 'It really was a heavenly day—it was all so beautiful.'

Mr Rijnma ter Salis stood looking at her for a moment, and then gathered her into his arms and unhurriedly kissed her surprised mouth. 'Indeed it was, Eugenie, and you are so beautiful too.'

He pushed open the lobby doors, and the porter woke up and got to his feet as Mr Rijnma ter Salis went away back to the car without so much as a backward glance.

Eugenie wished the porter goodnight and wandered up to her room. She had been kissed on a number of occasions by men, pleasant casual kisses quickly forgotten, but Mr Rijnma ter Salis had made sure that she wasn't going to forget his. Did he kiss Saphira like that, she wondered, and was it because he missed the horrible creature that he had kissed Eugenie?

'I shall ask him tomorrow,' she muttered, getting ready for bed. But she had to admit that she had enjoyed it.

She was by no means a timid girl, but even she baulked at asking him any such thing the next morning. He greeted her at breakfast in exactly the manner he used when he was about to do a ward round; to do more than comment upon the fine day was beyond her. He agreed gravely with her, made civil conversation with Mevrouw van Tegge and excused himself with the plea that he wished to make a final check on his patient.

When he had gone Mevrouw van Tegge said very comfortably, 'I dare say you will wish to say goodbye to everyone at the hospital. Would you like the car to take you there?'

Eugenie said that she would walk. On the way back she intended to buy some of the dragon flowers; they would be awkward to carry but they would look delightful in her room in Groningen. They were leaving directly after lunch; she was to be ready at half-past one. She had the morning before her. She walked to the hospital, bade goodbye to everyone she had known there, including her patient, and then wandered through the streets, spending her last escudos. The dragon flowers were indeed bulky, but they had been well wrapped; she would take them in the plane with her and Mr Rijnma ter Salis would just have to put up with them. She had coffee in a restaurant near the sea-front, fending off friendly young men who wished to keep her company, and presently she returned to the consulate to eat an early lunch with a coolly friendly Mr Rijnma ter Salis and their hostess. He remained friendly, though somewhat cooler when he saw the dragon flowers and the various parcels and packages she had acquired, but he stowed them in the car, waited while she bade Mevrouw van Tegge goodbye and drove to the airport. Jan van Daal was waiting for them, leading them away from the reception area towards a corner of the airport where there were several smaller planes lined up.

'Are we going in one of these?' asked Eugenie.

Jan answered her. 'Government business,' he told her, 'and very much quicker.' He eyed her considerable luggage. 'A good thing, there'll be room for your parcels and flowers.' He gave her a serious smile. 'Did you manage to get to that museum?'

'No, I didn't have the time.' She smiled at him in her friendly way. 'But next time I come I'll certainly make it the first place I go to see.'

'Good. We could go together. I look forward to that.'

Mr Rijnma ter Salis had been standing silently listening. 'A pleasing prospect for both of you,' he commented suavely. 'Eugenie, shall we load your luggage?'

The flight was uneventful. Mr Rijnma ter Salis immersed himself in a pile of papers, first of all handing her an armful of magazines and newspapers, pausing only to offer her coffee from a thermos flask after an hour or so. She read the magazines from cover to cover and then sat looking out of the porthole at the sea far below until they were over land. She stared down at that too, but since she had no idea where they were it might just as well have been the Atlantic.

She was offered more coffee and sandwiches presently, asked if she were quite comfortable, and left once more to her own devices, so she got out a pen and the back of her diary and began to do some sums. She had spent most of the money she had brought with her but she still had a nice little nest-egg. She would go home for a few weeks when she went back to England, and take her time about finding a job not too far away. She paused in her arithmetic to contemplate the future. She had ignored it while they had been in Madeira but now it had to be faced. Never seeing him again was something she had to face, but not just yet. There were, hopefully, still several more weeks before his new theatre sister would replace her. It was very evident that now that they were returning to Groningen they would resume their working relationship. Their wonderful day in Madeira had been nothing but a pleasant episode to him, already forgotten no doubt with the prospect of an early meeting with his Saphira. Eugenie frowned. Drat the girl!

They were over Holland, speeding towards Groningen, when he spoke. 'If you're not too tired tomorrow, I shall want you in the afternoon. A nervous lady—she needs a pacemaker. She insists upon seeing everyone connected with the operation before she will undergo it. One o'clock at the hospital.'

At her look of surprise, he added, 'She is rather an important person . . .'

'Very well, sir. Where am I to go?'

'To my rooms. I'll let you have the address.'

He sounded remote. Probably thinking about his Saphira, thought Eugenie. Perhaps she would be at the airport. They touched down well away from the main building and the car was waiting for them, driven by a neatly dressed well built man, who greeted Mr Rijnma ter Salis with polite familiarity. There was no Saphira. She would be waiting for him at home, wherever that was . . .

Bidden to do so, Eugenie got into the car beside Mr Rijnma ter Salis and was driven without loss of time to the hospital, where he got out of the car, handed her various packages and suitcase to the porter, reminded her not to be late on the following day, and drove himself away with the man—Jaap, if she had heard correctly—sitting beside him.

Well, she thought, making her way to her room, that's that and very nice while it lasted. Now to forget all about it.

Easier said than done; she presented herself on duty at one o'clock precisely feeling wretchedly unhappy. It would have been so much easier to forget if he hadn't kissed her—and in such a fashion.

Zuster Corsma greeted her pleasantly. 'It is nice to have you back and I hear everything was most satisfactory. You enjoyed your visit to Madeira?' She didn't wait for an answer. 'You are to go to the front entrance—there is a car there. You will be taken to Mr Rijnma ter Salis's consulting-rooms, and when you are no longer needed you will be driven back here. You will be on duty when you come back until night staff come on.' She peered at the off-duty rota on her desk. 'There are no cases on Saturday or Sunday; you may have your days off then. On Monday there is an anterior thoracotomy—a thickened pericardium—a pacemaker to be replaced, and on the day following a valve replacement. There is also a baby with a valvular lesion. It hasn't been decided yet if and when anything can be done. Now run along or you'll be late.'

At least she would be kept busy, reflected Eugenie, nipping smartly to the entrance. Jaap was there, standing by a Rover. He wished her good day and she got in beside him, refusing to sit on the back seat by herself. 'I expect you speak English?' she asked hopefully.

He did, heavily accented but fluent enough.

'You work for Mr Rijnma ter Salis?' she asked.

He told her that he did, had done for many years, and that his wife was housekeeper. She longed to ask more but didn't dare, and they talked about the weather, the sights of Groningen that he said she must be sure to see before she went back to

England, and the weather again. By that time he had stopped the car in a wide street lined with tall houses, got out, ushered her on to the pavement and led her to a heavy door with an enormous brass knocker. He didn't thump it though, but produced a key, opened the door and told her to go up the stairs to the first floor, and closed the door behind her.

The hall was high-ceilinged and narrow with the staircase set in the wall on one side. She went up slowly, looking around her as she went, and on the landing above she stood for a moment, reading the names on the four doors there. All doctors, she presumed, and Mr Rijnma ter Salis's name was on the end one, only he was a professor. He might have said so, she thought vexedly as she opened it.

A waiting-room, she supposed, for there were chairs scattered about and small tables with magazines on them under the high windows. A woman was sitting at a desk. She looked severe, with grey hair strained back from a long face, but her smile was nice. 'Zuster Spencer? I'll let him know you're here.' Her English was almost accentless, and Eugenie, stumbling over the few Dutch words she had managed to learn, felt envy.

'Go on in,' said the severe woman encouragingly, so Eugenie opened the door pointed out to her, and went in.

Mr Rijnma ter Salis was sitting at his desk, writing, but he got to his feet as she went in. 'Ah, sit down, Eugenie—my patient will be here very shortly and when we have finished our talk I want you to go back with her to the hospital, show her something of the theatre block—you'll find the anaesthetist and my registrar there. Stay with her while they talk to her and see her safely back into her car. If you think this is highly unusual, it is, but she is rather a special patient.'

She couldn't think of anything to say, and after a moment he told her who it was. 'Someone of such international repute naturally wishes to remain incognito. Illness is something the famous don't acknowledge.'

'Then why must she see us and Theatre? Why does she want to meet us?'

He smiled a little. 'Because she is terrified; meeting us and talking to us may help her to take a more rational view of the operation.'

He got up and went over to the window and looked out. 'You enjoyed our stay in Madeira?'

'Very much.' She tried to sound pleasantly cool and spoilt it by blushing.

He didn't appear to notice. 'A successful case. You did very well, Eugenie, you are a very calm person.'

There was no point in contradicting him, and she was saved from making conversation by the entrance of his patient.

The next hour or so were trying. If that is being famous, thought Eugenie, then I'll stay as I am. The patient was beautiful and charming and completely obsessed with herself. Eugenie watched Mr Rijnma ter Salis charm her in his turn into an acceptance of the operation and a period out of the public eye, and she admired his tact and his monumental patience. The anaesthetist was at his most soothing, backed up by Zuster Corsma and the registrar, and the lady went at last, convinced that

she was a model of high-minded courage and
bidding them goodbye with the graciousness of
royalty.

'I am glad,' said Zuster Corsma, 'that we seldom
have patients such as this lady. You will scrub for
Mr Rijnma ter Salis, of course, Sister Spencer.'

The rest of the week was easy. Mr Rijnma ter Salis
didn't come in at all and the registrars, dealing with
pacemakers and angiocardiographies, gave no hint
as to where he was. Eugenie went off duty on Friday
night feeling frustrated. She tried not to think of
him enjoying himself somewhere with his Saphira,
and pondered over her weekend. Sunday she had
already planned more or less—a visit to the St
Martinikerk and a tour on foot of the city, a snack
lunch in one of its many coffee shops, and an
afternoon in the Prinsenhof gardens, tea—an elegant tea, she thought—in one of the hotels and
then back to the hospital. Monday was going to be
a long day...

Saturday was a different matter. There was a
great deal to see in Groningen but it was a chance
to see something of the surrounding country. She
would take a bus; she had a timetable and the names
of some of the towns were very intriguing. She decided on Heiligerlee for no other reason than that
its name appealed to her. There were buses to
Winschoten close by and, as far as she could see,
it was on or near a main road. Twenty-three miles
was no distance and there was a train service as
well...

Having arranged her weekend to her satisfaction, she spent a cheerful evening in the pleasant

sitting-room with her colleagues off duty, watching on television first of all an American film with subtitles, which made it hard to follow since the text in a strange language prevented her from listening to the characters. Then there was an interview— one serious elderly man questioning another equally serious man, talking, as far as she was concerned, nonsense.

# CHAPTER SIX

EUGENIE planned to catch a bus just before eleven o'clock. She would be in Heiligerlee by midday and spend the afternoon there, returning in the early evening to find somewhere quiet to eat in Groningen. First though she needed to do some shopping, soap and toothpaste and shampoo and, if she saw something suitable, a present or two. She went out early into the busy streets and found the morning warm and sunny. She did some shopping, took her purchases back to her room and went back into the streets again. There was time for coffee before the bus went . . .

It was disappointing to find that the sky had become overcast while she had been in the café. The sky was still blue overhead but it looked metallic, although there were no clouds to be seen in the strip of sky above her head between the tall houses. She walked briskly, anxious not to miss her bus, her head full of Mr Rijnma ter Salis. She wondered where he was and what he was doing. Miles away for all she knew.

The Bentley came to a quiet halt beside her and he opened the door. 'Where are you off to?' he wanted to know.

The suddenness of it had paled her cheeks and roused her temper, even though life had suddenly become wonderful. 'You shouldn't creep up on me like that,' she told him sharply. 'I'm going to catch a bus...'

'Then get in. I'll drop you off at the bus station.'

'You're very kind, but I can walk—it's not far.'

She was uneasily aware as she spoke that the sky had darkened and there were slow, heavy drops of rain falling. 'There's not any need...'

There was a vivid flash of lightning and on its heels a majestic peal of thunder, and at the same time it rained, not Shakespeare's gentle rain but a cloudburst. Eugenie, who had a childlike fear of thunder and lightning, shot into the car as though a giant hand had propelled her from behind. With her eyes tightly shut, she said unnecessarily, 'I'm afraid of storms.' She gave a small squeak as an awe-inspiring clap of thunder subsided slowly into a menacing mutter.

Mr Rijnma ter Salis's voice was comforting. 'We do get some rather bad storms here. You can catch the next bus. In the meantime let me offer you a cup of coffee.'

She opened a cautious eye. 'Sorry to be such a fool. I'll be quite all right now. Here's the bus depot...'

He drove past it. 'The storm is by no means over,' he pointed out, and obligingly a flash of lightning flared. 'Far better wait for a while. It won't last long.'

He drove unconcernedly through the downpour, past the Martinikerk and the heart of the city, past lovely old houses and canals, and Eugenie, feeling safe now, asked sharply, 'Where have you been? It's days...'

He said gently, 'There are three hospitals in Groningen, Eugenie. I have clinics in all three of them, although I only operate in one.'

'Well, it's not my business,' she muttered, and caught her breath at another flash of lightning. The storm was right overhead now.

The street ran alongside a canal with great gabled houses facing the water. Mr Rijnma ter Salis parked the car halfway down it and got out.

'Where's this?' she wanted to know as he opened her door to help her out.

'I live here.'

There was no point in standing and arguing on the narrow pavement, for it was still teeming down. She allowed herself to be urged up the double steps and in through the solid door, stout enough to withstand a siege.

There was a lobby and glass doors opening into a wide hall, its walls panelled with dark wood, its floor black and white marble. There was a crystal chandelier hanging from the ceiling and a staircase with carved wooden balustrade at the far end.

'Your feet are wet,' observed Mr Rijnma ter Salis. 'Take off your sandals. Mientje will dry them.'

She did as she was told and put a hand to her hair.

'Never mind that, come and have some coffee.' He turned as he spoke, and a tall, stout woman swept through a door at the back of the hall to meet them.

'Ah, Mientje——' He lapsed into Dutch for a moment, then said, 'Eugenie, this is Mientje, my housekeeper.'

Eugenie offered a hand and said, 'How do you do?' in her friendly way; one of the nurses at the hospital had told her the Dutch equivalent but she wasn't going to have him laughing at her clumsy attempts to pronounce his language. Anyway Mientje seemed to understand, judging by her smile.

Somewhere behind the door at the back of the hall there was a dog barking. Eugenie turned a questioning look upon her host.

'That's Butch. You shall see him presently.' He nodded to his housekeeper, took Eugenie by the arm and ushered her through one of the doors in the hall. The room was very splendid, with a high plastered ceiling, silk-hung walls and tall windows. A room for giants, but then Mr Rijnma ter Salis was very nearly that. There were vast wing-back chairs, two sofas flanking the fireplace, great glass-fronted cabinets along the walls and mahogany tripod tables placed exactly where they were wanted most. There were two vastly tall windows draped in mulberry satin and an enormous silk carpet covering most of the wooden floor.

'Oh, how lovely!' exclaimed Eugenie, and then drew a sharp breath as Saphira rose from a chair and strolled towards them.

She gave Eugenie a wintry smile and addressed herself to Mr Rijnma ter Salis in Dutch.

He answered her in English. 'Ah, Saphira—a delightful surprise. We shall all have coffee together. I have brought Eugenie back with me to shelter until the storm is over.' He offered Eugenie a chair and sat down in a great wing chair, facing the two of them. His manner was mild as milk.

Eugenie sought for a suitable topic of conversation. She asked politely, 'Your dog Butch—what breed is he? Can I see him?'

'His ancestry is mixed, I'm afraid. Certainly you shall see him before you go. Saphira finds dogs— and cats—tiresome in the house, so he is banished to the kitchen when she is here.'

Saphira smoothed the skirt of her cashmere two-piece. 'They ruin my clothes.' She cast a disparaging look at Eugenie's denim skirt, her eyes travelling upwards to the blouse and Marks and Spencer cardigan. 'Of course, if clothes don't matter...'

How rude, thought Eugenie. I'd like to shake her. Instead she smiled with great sweetness. 'Well, they don't really, do they? Not with animals and children. They're rather a waste of time too.'

Mr Rijnma ter Salis kept a straight face. 'Presumably one dresses to suit the occasion,' he observed placidly, then added, 'Ah, here is the coffee.'

The man who had driven Eugenie to Mr Rijnma ter Salis's rooms was carrying the tray. He bade her good morning and smiled as he set the tray down on the small table between them. He hesitated when Saphira spoke sharply to him, and glanced at his master.

Mr Rijnma ter Salis's voice was quiet—Eugenie wished she could understand what he was saying— something which made Saphira bite her lip and look angry. She got up though and poured the coffee, and he gave Eugenie a cup before taking his own. Settling in his chair once more, he asked, 'Where do you plan to go, Eugenie?'

'Heiligerlee—there's a good bus service.'

'Why should you want to go there? There's nothing,' said Saphira.

'I like the name.'

'As good a reason as any for visiting a place,' observed Mr Rijnma ter Salis. 'They make bells there, did you know? Send them all over the world. It's a small town but pretty; you will enjoy it.'

The storm was passing. There was an occasional flash of lightning and a rumble of thunder, but the sky was no longer overcast. Eugenie put down her coffee-cup. 'It was kind of you to let me shelter here,' she told him in her friendly way. 'I'm sure I'm going to enjoy my trip and it's getting fine again.'

She got to her feet and Mr Rijnma ter Salis stood up. 'Come and see Butch before you go?'

She smiled at Saphira. 'Goodbye. I hope I haven't interrupted your morning.'

Saphira shrugged. 'Enjoy your day. On your own, I suppose?'

A remark not worth answering, Eugenie considered.

Mr Rijnma ter Salis led the way across the hall and through a door beside the stairs. There were a few steps down, then another door which he opened on to a vast kitchen. She sighed with delight at the sight of it—a flagstoned floor, a vast dresser loaded with dishes, giant soup tureens and rows of plates, a very up-to-date Aga which fitted into its old-fashioned surroundings, and a great table in the centre ringed around by ladderback chairs. There were copper saucepans on the shelves and a pleasant clutter of vegetables piled on the table. Mientje was standing there, and two girls were standing at the vast sink at the other end of the kitchen, washing china. They stopped what they were doing as Mr Rijnma ter Salis and Eugenie went in, and then resumed their work at a word from Mientje.

Mr Rijnma ter Salis said something to make them all laugh and turned to fend off the delighted greeting from Butch, a dog of such varied ancestry it was impossible to describe him—the size of a Labrador with a woolly coat, a foxy face, and soulful eyes at variance with a formidable set of teeth.

Eugenie knelt down to speak to him. 'You're beautiful,' she told him, 'a bit of all the best kind of dogs.'

Butch closed his eyes and sighed happily as she scratched the top of his woolly head.

'He doesn't have to live in the kitchen, does he?' she asked.

'Certainly not, he has the run of the house.' Mr Rijnma ter Salis was lounging against the kitchen table.

'But when you are married...' She caught his eye and didn't finish the sentence.

'I never cross my bridges until I get to them,' he told her blandly.

She got up then and went to the door, bade Mientje goodbye, and went back into the hall with him at her heels. She stopped then and offered a hand. 'Thank you again, I'm most grateful.'

He went to the door with her and opened it. 'Dartmoor seems a long way away,' he observed. 'Do you wish that you were there?'

'I do miss it,' she acknowledged, 'but I like being here.'

'Why?'

She avoided his stare. 'Oh—all sorts of reasons.' She had got herself out of the door and on to the steps. 'Goodbye, sir.'

His hand held her. 'Do I seem so old to you that I have to be addressed as "sir" with every other breath?'

'You're not old—whatever made you think that? Only you're—you're a consultant. I don't *think* of you as sir, you know.'

He smiled slowly. 'Enjoy your day, Eugenie.'

She caught her bus and spent the rest of the day at Heiligerlee, looking at the bells, strolling round the streets, admiring the houses, eating lunch in a small café, trying out her few words of Dutch. She took the bus back in the early afternoon, trying to decide what she should do with her evening. To go back to the hospital was to waste several hours of her day; on the other hand she was dubious about eating in a restaurant on her own. She could, of course, go to a cinema. She stood at the bus depot, uncertain.

'How very fortunate that I should find you here,' observed Mr Rijnma ter Salis, looming over her head and giving her a fright. 'Take pity on me and keep me company for a few hours,' and before she could speak he added, 'Saphira has gone to a dinner-dance but I need to stay at home in case I'm wanted.'

She studied his face and then said carefully, 'I was going back to the hospital.'

'Ah—then you will take pity on me if you have nothing better to do. I do dislike eating alone.'

She believed him. 'Well, so do I—especially in a foreign country.'

'Splendid. I was walking—it isn't far.'

'Somewhere quite quiet, please,' she begged him. 'I'm not dressed up and I've been walking around—I'm untidy.'

'Somewhere quiet it shall be.'

It took her a moment or two to realise that they were going to his house. She stopped in the middle of the pavement and gave him an enquiring look, but before she could speak he forestalled her. 'You don't mind? If I should be called away—you can't imagine how time is wasted looking for me if I should be wanted.' His voice held just the right amount of casual interest. 'Besides, it will give me a chance to discuss Monday's list. There are one or two things...'

So she walked on; put like that it seemed reasonable enough and she was hungry. Besides, it was an unexpected happiness to be with him. If I had been Saphira, she reflected, I'd have refused to go out without him...

Mr Rijnma ter Salis, watching her face with a seemingly casual glance, had a shrewd idea of what she was thinking. His own thoughts were just as busy but nothing of them showed in his face.

Mientje, appealed to when they reached the house, promised a nice little dinner within an hour and Jaap led Eugenie away up the staircase to a pretty bedroom so that she might tidy herself. High time too, thought Eugenie, surveying herself in the dressing-table glass. Her hair was woefully untidy, and her face needed attention. She set to work to repair the damage and ten minutes later went back

downstairs, her hair very neat, her lovely face carefully made up. She wished that she had a pretty
dress on and then decided that sadly it wouldn't
matter what she wore, for Mr Rijnma ter Salis never
seemed to look at her—really look. She was of
course mistaken.

They were joined by Butch in the drawing-room,
sitting between them as they had their drinks and
presently accompanying them to the dining-room
where they dined off mushroom soup, duck with
black cherry sauce and then Dutch apple pie with
a great deal of whipped cream. Eugenie wondered
if Mr Rijnma ter Salis always dined in such
splendour with a linen and lace cloth and lovely old
silver and crystal, or if it was just because she was
there. Somehow she had always imagined him
eating alone at an austere table, probably with a
book propped before him—that was, of course,
unless Saphira was with him.

That lady wasn't mentioned; they talked about
a great many matters, none of them personal and
none of them particularly serious, but she was delighted to find that they shared the same taste in
books and music, hadn't much time for television
and liked walking in the rain. It was the first time,
she thought, that they had really talked; she felt
very much at ease with him which of course
wouldn't do at all. On Monday she must remember
that—it would be easier in uniform...

They went back to the drawing-room presently
and sat over their coffee, with Butch snoozing with
his eyes closed in his foxy face, his chin resting on
his master's shoes. The ebony bracket clock on the
wide ledge above the fireplace tinkling the hour,

echoed by the slow gentle chimes of the long-case clock in the hall, stopped her in mid-sentence.

'It's ten o'clock—I had no idea—your whole evening—I shouldn't have stayed so long! I do hope you hadn't planned anything.'

She had got to her feet, a little flustered but still her usual sensible self. He stood up too but without haste. 'A delightful evening—I am so grateful that you stayed to keep me company and, believe me, I had no plans to do anything. I'll drive you back to the hospital.'

On the way back he didn't ask her what she intended to do on Sunday and she was thankful for that; he might have felt that she expected an invitation to something or other, although on second thoughts she was sure that Saphira would never allow that.

She spent Sunday exactly as she had planned and if she wished for company she didn't allow herself to brood over it. The other sisters at the hospital were friendly and helpful but she had been there too short a time to have become really friendly with any of them and, as Zuster Corsma explained when she went on duty on Monday morning, Mr Rijnma ter Salis's theatre sister didn't work the same rigid hours as the resident sisters. That was the whole idea, she explained in her careful English. He might be sent for at any moment of the day or night and she must be prepared to go with him and stay for as long as was necessary. 'You are here for weeks in this hospital and then all at once you are somewhere else.'

She nodded rather severely. 'Until now you are satisfactory, I think. Go now and check the theatre—he will be here in half an hour and it will be a long case. You will, of course, scrub.'

She was standing surrounded by her trolleys, the patient on the table, when he came into Theatre, bade her a cool good morning and began his work. She hadn't expected more than that, but she had been taken aback by the coldness of his eyes over his mask. She forgot it immediately, concentrating upon her work. It was four hours before the patient left Theatre and he went to Intensive Care with him, leaving Eugenie and her staff to clear up and ready Theatre for the next case, listed for the late afternoon. Mr Rijnma ter Salis wasn't operating again until Wednesday; she supposed that she would scrub for anything which the registrar might need to do.

Which was exactly what she did.

The baby with a valvular lesion was well enough for an operation on Wednesday, but it was a delicate matter which needed skill and patience. It was successful; Eugenie went off duty with the pleasant feeling that those concentrated few hours in Theatre had been well worth while.

Mr Rijnma ter Salis had thanked her as he left Theatre and she had murmured composedly. He had no more cases that week and she took a long look at his calm face, since that look would have to last her for a few days. He had been perfectly civil but the easy bonhomie they had enjoyed was no longer there. She went off duty with the prospect of two more free days at the end of the week and with no idea of how to spend them. She would have to get out her guidebook and make more plans...

Plans, however, were made for her, with a suddenness which took her breath away. She was actually in her dressing-gown, ready for bed, when she was called to the telephone.

'We are leaving for Bosnia at eight o'clock tomorrow morning,' said Mr Rijnma ter Salis. He sounded as though he were telling her to catch the seventy-three bus to Marble Arch. 'Uniform—you'll be given suitable kit on board the plane. There are two patients too ill to fly out without surgery. Shrapnel wounds. Both children. Raf van Groot will be with us, and a technician. I shall want my instruments packed and put with the plasma and the rest of the equipment. See to that, will you? You'll be collected at seven o'clock tomorrow morning.'

He rang off, leaving her with her mouth open. After a moment she went to her room and got back into her uniform. After all, that was what she was here for, she reminded herself, bundling her hair up anyhow under its cap.

Zuster Corsma was still on duty, handing over to the night staff. Eugenie explained why she had returned and listened resignedly to that lady repeating what she had already told herself—that that was what she was there for—before going away to deal with the instruments.

It took some time to check them and she was hindered by Raf van Groot, the anaesthetist, who advised her cheerfully that they would have to deal with the patients in far from perfect conditions. 'We shall probably be shelled and shot at too,' she was told cheerfully.

She finished what she was doing, checked that the equipment was all ready, that the plasma was there together with extra drains, tubes, needles and catgut and then, being a sensible girl, went in search of instant coffee, tins of milk and a Thermos flask. She had no doubt that they would be fed, but Mr Rijnma ter Salis wasn't likely to stop for a meal once he got started; if he intended to operate on the two cases one after the other then a hot drink would be necessary. He might be a giant of a man, but he'd have to stop some time, and so would she, for that matter.

It was late by the time she had showered and got into bed. The news of their journey had spread and a constant stream of her fellow-workers came to talk to her about it. The last one to go asked, 'Are you afraid, Eugenie?'

'I haven't had time yet,' said Eugenie, 'but I expect I shall be terrified.'

She was up and dressed and eating her breakfast in a still empty canteen by half-past six. She had crammed her shoulder-bag with undies, a towel, toothpaste, soap, hairbrush, shampoo, and passport and the small amount of money she had with her. She had no idea what she might need and Mr Rijnma ter Salis hadn't told her. Probably he hadn't given it a thought. In any case, once he had operated and the patients were well enough to move, they would be brought back to Groningen—the sooner the better.

She wasn't hungry but it was sensible to eat something. She chewed bread and butter and cheese, drank the coffee a sleepy girl brought, and went to the entrance.

His good morning was brisk but he eyed her shoulder-bag with some doubt. 'We may be there for several days.'

'Yes. I expected that. I've all I need with me.'

He tossed the bag on to the back seat with a lift of the eyebrows which brought the colour to her cheeks. 'No petticoats?' he asked.

'No petticoats,' said Eugenie, and got into the car and sat composedly while he stowed things away.

He got in beside her presently, the epitome of leisure in his casual trousers and open-necked shirt. She said snappily, 'I hope you will have the time to tell me where we are going and how and for how long.' She was looking ahead, intent on keeping distantly polite.

'I'm not surprised that you are getting peevish. Do vent your spleen upon me if it will help.' He gave her a quick sidelong glance. 'We are to be flown out in an air force plane from an airfield outside the city. You will be given battle dress to wear and will change before we leave. There are two children, as I told you. I'll operate if possible, and we may have to stay a day or two. As soon as it is safe to fly them out, that will be done.'

He was driving through the early morning streets, his manner as nonchalant as if he were going on a picnic. 'Once we're aboard I'll go over the cases with you. Van Groot and Wim are to meet us at the airport.'

They were out in the country now with the green placid fields all around them. She would be glad to see them again, reflected Eugenie.

'Had you planned anything for the weekend?' he asked.

'No. I thought I would explore a bit,' she added. 'I phoned Mother last night but I didn't tell her where we were going.'

'Very sensible of you. I had a chat with your father. He agrees with me that there is no need for your mother to know where we are going. You can phone her when we get back.'

'Oh, well, thank you. He wasn't worried?'

'I told him that you would be in safe hands, Eugenie.'

'Thank you. I expect your Saphira is worried...' She hadn't known why she had said that, and waited uneasily for his reply.

'No. No, not worried. A little annoyed since we were to have been guests of friends in Limburg for the weekend. She will go on her own, though.'

Something in his voice made her say hastily, 'I dare say she understands—that is, when she is your wife she will get used to your being away from home.' She plodded on, very anxious to sound sympathetic without being nosy. 'Doctors' wives— I mean, you're away a lot, aren't you?'

'Indeed I am——' his voice was silky '—but you have no need to worry about me, Eugenie.'

'I'm not in the least worried about you, sir. Why should I be?'

'An interesting question.'

He slowed the car and stopped at a guarded gate, spoke to the sentry and then drove on. There were several buildings, hangars, she supposed, and what looked like a control tower and one or two severe red-brick edifices, presumably offices. Mr Rijnma ter Salis stopped beside these and got out and opened her door. 'Van Groot and Wim are here. Go through that first door; there'll be someone to tell you what to do.'

It was like being in a dream but since she was in it she might as well do as she was told without demur. She went through the door and a pretty girl in uniform said, 'Hello, I'm Sein. Your kit's here. You've got ten minutes.'

Eugenie followed her into a small room bare save for a couple of chairs and a table. 'Leave your stuff here,' said Sein. 'There's a looking-glass in the loo through that door. I hope everything fits—I did the best I could...'

Eugenie got into the camouflage trousers and shirt. The trousers were rather too big, but Sein found a belt to hold them secure and offered a blue helmet and a satchel. 'There'll be coffee on the plane,' she assured Eugenie.

'How long does it take to get there?'

'Oh, several hours. You've got a marvellous man to talk to, so you won't notice the time.' She smiled. 'I wouldn't mind being in your shoes.'

'He's going to marry a very beautiful young woman,' said Eugenie, 'and anyway I expect we shall only talk shop.' She saw the puzzled look on Sein's face. 'About the operation he hopes to do,' she explained.

'A pity. I think you must go now. Good luck!'

There was a jeep outside. Mr Rijnma ter Salis, Dr van Groot and Wim were already in it with the driver. Hands hauled her aboard and she was squashed between Mr Rijnma ter Salis and a pile of equipment. Dr van Groot and Wim wished her good morning, smiling and nodding for all the world as though they were in Theatre, waiting for the list to be started. Mr Rijnma ter Salis introduced her to the driver, who grinned at her with a cheerful hello and started the jeep. He drove to the furthest corner of the airfield where there was a plane, its engines already rumbling, and Eugenie was handed out and then handed into the plane by friendly hands.

'Sit here,' she was advised, and she settled thankfully in the functional interior. The pilot and his co-pilot introduced themselves while the others were supervising the loading of the equipment. 'Jake, and this is Evert—a pleasure to have you aboard, Sister. We don't often get beautiful ladies as passengers. Flown much, have you?'

'We had to fly to Madeira a week or two ago. I don't much care for flying.'

'We'll go carefully,' Jake assured her. 'Suck a sweet when we take off and then catch up on your beauty sleep. Not that you need to do that,' he added gallantly.

She laughed then because he had such a friendly face and Mr Rijnma ter Salis, climbing aboard, looked at her sharply. She had a lovely laugh.

Once they were airborne she did as Jake suggested and closed her eyes, only to open them again as Mr Rijnma ter Salis eased his vast person into the seat beside her.

'We'd better go over what facts we have,' he told her in a voice which dismissed any idea she might have had of having a snooze.

She sat up straight as he took out the notes he had made from his case, and listened carefully to

what he had to say. The plane was noisy and presumably it was turbulence which was sending it up
and down like a lift, but he didn't seem to notice.
She did her best to pretend to herself that she was
in the theatre block, listening to his instructions
before the list.

She peeped at his face as he bent over his papers.
He was in battle dress too and he looked years
younger, his shirt sleeves rolled up, the collar open.
He looked up very suddenly and stared at her and
she found that she couldn't take her eyes away from
him. Then he smiled slowly.

'Let's hope that we can make a good job of it.'
His hand rested lightly on hers for a moment. 'I'm
going to discuss things with van Groot. Close your
eyes, there will be coffee when you wake.'

It seemed good advice. Although she kept her
eyes shut she didn't sleep. She should be ashamed
of herself, she thought, feeling happy because she
was with him once more, when there were those
thousands of unhappy, ill people, some of whom
they would see presently.

She loved him so—a useless love that would never
come to anything, and in a few weeks her replacement would arrive and she would go back to
England and not see him again.

She sat there, hazy daydreams weaving around
her head, and presently she slept.

It was Wim who woke her with a mug of coffee
and a packet of sandwiches. 'Drink and eat,' he
told her in his very adequate school English. 'Soon
we arrive. You have slept well?'

She thanked him and looked at her watch. She
had indeed, for almost two hours. She drank the

coffee and bit into the sandwiches and peered out of the window. They were over land, but she had no idea which land; it all looked flat and thickly wooded.

Mr Rijnma ter Salis was there again, holding a sandwich in one hand. 'Feeling all right? Good. If you crane your neck you'll get a glimpse of the Adriatic. We've flown across Germany and Austria and we're almost there. We shall have to climb shortly. It's mountainous country, but we should touch down in half an hour or so, Jake says. We shall go straight to the hospital and see the surgeons. We might possibly operate later today.'

He got up. 'It will be as well if you stay with me while we talk.'

'Very well, Mr Rijnma ter Salis.'

'I think that it would be a good idea if you were to call me Aderik, don't you agree?'

'Very well, Mr... Aderik.'

She felt his hand on her shoulder, large and comforting, before he went back to the others.

Presently they landed and she was bustled into a jeep and driven together with the others to the airport buildings and, after a brief stop, they rattled on along a narrow road, full of potholes. Mountains rose on one side of it and on the other there were fields and several ruined farmhouses standing forlornly. They were driving through the outskirts of the town when a shell exploded several hundred yards away and Eugenie let out a startled 'Oh!' Mr Rijnma ter Salis, sitting across from her, leaned over and took her hand. He didn't say anything, didn't even look at her.

'There's a cease-fire,' he said comfortably. 'That must have been fired by mistake.'

Everyone laughed and she laughed too with only a very slight wobble. She didn't have to be scared. Aderik was here, close by her.

# CHAPTER SEVEN

IT was late by the time Eugenie went to the room she had been given at the hospital. She was tired, but not too tired to mull over the day. It had been a long one and one she would never forget. If it hadn't been for Aderik's presence, she thought she might have burst into tears and gone on weeping on and off all day. Obviously he hadn't expected her to do that; they were there on a job and personal feelings had nothing to do with it, so she had listened while the medical men talked, walked through the crowded ward to where the two children lay and then later, with Wim helping her, she had got the theatre ready. There had been nurses there too and she marvelled at their courage and the relief and delight when the medical stores they had brought with them were unpacked.

It had been quite late in the day when Mr Rijnma ter Salis operated. It had taken a long time to remove the tiny splinter of shrapnel lodged within a hair's breadth of the child's heart, but he had done it successfully. The child would recover and, as soon as it was feasible, would be flown out to another hospital and safety. The second child was, if that were possible, a more serious matter. There was a shell splinter in the heart itself; they would need the heart-lung machine for that and the child wouldn't be fit for operation for at least twelve hours. There was another busy day ahead for all of them. She curled up on the rather hard mattress and went to sleep.

She had expected to get up early but not at four o'clock in the morning. A nurse shook her awake. 'You must go to Theatre—there is a wounded man. At once, you understand. I shall be there also and two of our doctors.'

Eugenie shot into her shirt and trousers, bundled her hair up and tied it on top of her head and sped through the passages and corridors, to find Aderik, Dr van Groot and Wim already there, together with two surgeons and the nurses.

Mr Rijnma ter Salis turned to her as she went in.

'A nicked aorta. I'll try and stitch it; if not I'll have to do an excision and an end-to-end union. He'll be up in ten minutes or so—there's no time to waste.'

He went away then and she set to with the nurses. The theatre was ready but there were his own instruments, already sterile, to lay out as soon as she had scrubbed.

The patient was a young man unconscious and pale in the light of the emergency light Wim had rigged up. Eugenie hoped that they were in time...

Mr Rijnma ter Salis worked with speed, completely absorbed in his task. Eugenie, ably assisted by the other nurses, heaved a sigh of relief as he straightened up at length. 'I think he'll do.' He spoke to the surgeons who had scrubbed with him. 'He's young and pretty tough.'

The patient was borne away, the men left the theatre and Eugenie was left with her colleagues to clear up once more and have everything ready. The hospital was large but only one theatre was usable;

small emergencies were done on the wards or wherever there was room to see to the patient, and if they decided to operate on the second child they would have to work fast.

There was help enough; she saw to Mr Rijnma ter Salis's own instruments while the others got the theatre ready again and then bore her off to have a meal of coffee and bread and cheese.

She went back to her room presently to wash and put up her hair tidily.

There was no time for make-up—in any case it didn't seem right to bother with lipstick and powder. Back in Theatre again she was told that Mr Rijnma ter Salis would operate in the afternoon and in the meantime perhaps she would like to lend a hand around the ward. There was plenty to do; she changed dressings, made beds and bandaged, exchanging smiles with the patients since she couldn't understand them or they her.

There was soup for lunch, and Aderik came and sat beside her for a few minutes. 'I'll do that child in an hour's time. Had a busy morning?'

She put down her spoon. 'Yes. It's like being in a nightmare——' she gave him a questioning look. '—isn't it?'

'A nightmare could never be a nightmare if you are in it, Eugenie.'

They sat looking at each other, his eyes steady on her face, hers studying him with a puzzled frown. She said slowly, 'Oh...' and managed to look away. 'I'd better go and get started...'

He got up with her and went back to Dr van Groot and Wim, and she plunged into her preparations in her usual methodical way, trying to forget his words. What exactly had he meant? she wondered time and again.

She had not time to wonder presently. The operation was a lengthy one and complicated, especially as they lacked a good deal of equipment. Still, Mr Rijnma ter Salis went placidly ahead, ignoring the lack of this and that, making do where he had to without so much as a mutter. The child would live. He went off with the two surgeons who had been working with him to supervise the aftercare of his small patient, and Eugenie began the task of clearing up with the rest of the theatre staff. It took some time before they were satisfied that everything was ready for whatever might come next, and they all trooped down to drink coffee and eat their supper of stew. It was mostly potatoes and other vegetables but she could have eaten a horse. Some of her companions went off duty and were replaced by others, and she wondered if she could take some time off too. There had been a few stray shells during the day and some rifle fire, but it was quiet now and a lovely early evening. She was at the entrance, wondering which way to go, when Mr Rijnma ter Salis took her arm in a gentle grip.

'Not that way—there's a fairly sheltered garden at the back of the hospital.' He led her back inside and through a maze of corridors, opened a side door and revealed an overgrown garden, strewn with rubble. There were flowers there, though, struggling between the weeds and boulders, and the air was sweet.

They picked their way round its edge until they reached a tumbling stone wall. The view was splendid. 'It's so beautiful,' said Eugenie, 'and something smells gorgeous.'

'Thyme. I expect we shall return home in two days' time, Eugenie.'

'How?'

'Just as we came. We shall take some patients back with us.' He turned her round to face him, smiling down at her. 'Thank you, Eugenie,' he added, 'my love.'

She lost her breath at that. Then found it again to say quickly, 'Hadn't we better go back?'

'Of course. It's been a long day. There are several cases for tomorrow—now we have brought in some supplies there's a lot to be done. I'll be helping out and I'm sure you'll be found something to do.'

She must have dreamt it; she went back into the hospital with him and said good night. Even if he had said it, he must be regretting it by now.

Why had he called her his love? she wondered as she got ready for bed. Was he so filled with longing for his Saphira that he had forgotten for a moment that it was Eugenie he was talking to and not Saphira? It seemed likely. She hoped that the girl loved him as much as he loved her...

She saw very little of him until they were ready to leave, and on the return flight there were the patients to see to and make as comfortable as possible. The long flight seemed twice as long and Aderik was avoiding her...

It was a lengthy business transferring the patients to the waiting ambulances and since one of them was a toddler with a young tearful mother, hopelessly bewildered, Eugenie was told to go with her. Dr van Groot and Wim wished her a cheerful *tot ziens*, but Mr Rijnma ter Salis had called a careless, 'See you later, Eugenie.'

The ambulance had borne them away, not to the hospital she was at in Groningen but to a smaller one on the other side of the city. It was two hours or more before she was set down outside the familiar building where she was staying, and late evening. She was to go to the *directrice* as soon as she arrived and that lady told her, after a pleasant greeting, that she was to take two days off. 'Mr Rijnma ter Salis won't be operating for two days and he tells me that you have had to work very hard. Go and enjoy some leisure, Sister Spencer, I am sure you will enjoy it.'

Two days in which to pull herself together and present a serene face and a cool manner towards Aderik. Eugenie went off to her room, to recount her trip to various of the nurses off duty and then soak for hours in a hot bath and emerge red as a lobster, and drink endless mugs of coffee while she was plied with questions. When at last she got into bed, she fell asleep within seconds.

She had no idea what she was going to do with her two free days; she got up, made a sketchy breakfast in the little kitchen at the end of the corridor, dressed and then sat on her bed, studying the map of the city. Coffee, she decided, then museums, lunch somewhere nice and some window-shopping in the afternoon. Tomorrow she would be more adventurous....

She found the coffee delicious and she had it in the company of two of the nurses who were off duty that morning. They parted company presently since they had to go on duty, and she spent the next

hour or so in the municipal museum, studying an-
tiquities, porcelain and paintings and all the while
thinking about Aderik. He would, of course, be
with Saphira; she tried very hard not to think about
him and found it impossible. What would they be
doing, she wondered—planning their wedding?

Mr Rijnma ter Salis was certainly with Saphira but
the subject of a wedding was the last thing being
discussed. Saphira had driven up in her smart little
sports car, defying the ruling that only essential cars
might drive through the city, and swanned into the
house as though she were already its mistress, and
now she was sitting opposite him, a delightful
picture in a vividly patterned silk dress, her hair an
artful tangle which only a really good hairdresser
could achieve, her make-up impeccable.

'If you aren't working today,' she said petu-
lantly, 'I can't think why you can't come with me
to den Haag. I should have thought that you would
have been delighted to come after those dreary days
away. Why you had to go I can't imagine—there
must be plenty of other surgeons.'

She eyed his bland face. 'Did you take that girl
with you?' When he nodded she added, 'I can't
think why—there must be dozens of nurses who
could do her work.'

When he didn't answer she asked, 'When is her
replacement coming?'

'Within the next week or so. I'm sorry I can't
come with you, Saphira—I've a good deal of work
to do even though I'm not at the hospital.'

Butch, who had been sitting at his master's feet, growled softly and Saphira said pettishly, 'Oh, for heaven's sake get rid of that dog. I can't stand him.'

'You know as well as I that I shall never get rid of Butch,' Mr Rijnma ter Salis said calmly. 'Offer my regrets to the van Hoeves, will you? I dare say they have planned a delightful day.'

Saphira got up. 'I sometimes wonder if marrying you is what I want. You get so little fun out of life.'

He looked as though he were going to reply but he said nothing, only saw her to his door and wished her a very pleasant day.

When she had gone he drove to the hospital with Butch sitting beside him. There was no need for him to be there since his registrar had already phoned him about his patients. All the same, he went to see them briefly, had coffee with Zuster Corsma and then went without haste to the front hall. 'Sister Spencer?' he enquired of the head porter. 'Has she gone out yet?'

'Half an hour ago,' he was told. 'Told her how to get to the municipal museum. She wanted to know where she could hire a bike, too. I told her to go to that place beside the station.'

Mr Rijnma ter Salis said, 'Oh, yes?' in an absent-minded fashion and got back into his car. 'How do you fancy a pleasant walk in the woods?' he wanted to know of Butch. 'We need soothing, you and I.'

Butch rolled his eyes and hung out his tongue, panting with pleasure at the treat in store.

The museum was almost empty of people. Aderik found Eugenie easily enough, sitting in front of some rather splendid old Dutch masters. She looked quite beautiful, sitting there so still in her cotton dress, her hands tidily in her lap, apparently absorbed in the paintings before her.

He sat down beside her, ignored her gasp of surprise and said, 'It's far too lovely a day to spend in a museum, and Butch is longing for a good tramp in the country. Would you come with us?'

She had got back her breath and regained her poise. 'That's very kind of you, but I'm really very happy here.'

'Don't talk rubbish.' He swept her to her feet and marched her along to the entrance, where she came to a halt.

'Where is your Saphira?' she asked severely.

'Gone to den Haag to a luncheon party and a dress show.'

She eyed him thoughtfully. 'Surely you would wish to be with her...?'

'Not at a dress show.'

'Oh, well ... all the same I don't think I should come with you.' She looked away, 'If I were Saphira, I should mind.'

'However, you aren't Saphira. Eugenie!'

She looked up at him. 'Yes?'

'Trust me?'

'Of course.'

'Good. The car is just across the street.'

Butch greeted her with delight, removed himself to the back seat and pressed a wet nose into the back of her neck. Feeling rather as though she had lost control of events, she settled into her seat as Aderik got in beside her.

'There's a delightful town called Ter Apel not too far away, south-east of here. There's a forest and some delightful walks. Butch needs to stretch his legs and so do I, and I think you might enjoy it.'

Eugenie had thrown common sense to the winds. 'It sounds lovely.' She turned to smile at him and then looked away quickly because he was smiling too—he had smiled liked that when he had called her his love.

Although of course I'm not, she told herself silently.

Ter Apel was about thirty-six miles from Groningen but Aderik didn't take the main roads; he drove to the Noordlaardermeer, alive with yachts, and then followed the country roads, never far from a canal, stopping at a village café for coffee while Butch took an airing.

Ter Apel was a large village where he parked the car. 'There's a medieval monastery not too far away if you feel like a walk.'

Eugenie had given herself over to the delights of the day, never mind Saphira. She nipped out of the car and the three of them set off through the beech forest, found the monastery, admired its ancient cloister and presently went back to the car.

'It's very pretty country here,' said Eugenie, intent on making polite conversation.

'Charming,' he agreed blandly. 'There are several villages just as pretty—we'll have lunch at one of them.'

They got into the car again and drove north for a few miles to Bourtange within a mile or two of the German border, where there was a charming little inn—a former seventeenth-century farmhouse—where they ate *uitsmijters*, eggs fried on layers of ham or cheese arranged on slices of buttered bread, and since it was quite a warm day they drank Pils, a light beer which Eugenie, who hadn't drunk beer before, found excellent. 'I hope it won't go to my head,' she observed, and was reassured when he ordered a pot of coffee at the end of their meal.

They were sitting outside the little place and there were few people around. Butch, comfortably full after his own slice of bread and butter and a bowl of water, slept between them and a few birds came to peck at the crumbs.

'Do you suppose they'll do?' asked Eugenie suddenly.

He understood her at once. 'Yes, I believe so. They can have the proper treatment and after-care now that they have some supplies. I'll let you know when they come to Holland—or of course they may go to England or anywhere else—but I shall be kept informed, I have no doubt.'

'I'd like to know. It's something I suppose I shall always remember.'

'Of course.' He glanced at her. 'Your replacement will be joining me very shortly. I expect you will be glad to go back to England?'

She said with hollow enthusiasm. 'Oh, of course. Although I have liked being here. Besides, I went to Madeira and then this last trip...'

'I dare say you may well have to travel again before you leave. I've a couple of patients next week in Groningen so you won't be idle.' He smiled at her. 'If you're not tired, we'll drive north—there's a delightful village—Warffum—a terp village with houses built on mounds above water level.'

He drove to Winschoten, took the road to Appingedam and then followed the coastline to the village. There was a museum there too, but he took her instead to see the church with its narrow radiating paths to the village. He knew his local history well, answering her questions patiently until presently he suggested that it was time for them to return.

Groningen was only fourteen miles away. As they entered the fringes of the city she said, 'It was very kind of you, Mr Rijnma ter Salis . . .'

'Aderik'.

'Well, Aderik, but only when we're not in hospital. I've had a lovely day.'

'Good.' She waited for him to say that he had enjoyed himself too but he didn't. He drove through the traffic-free streets and stopped before his house.

'Tea?' He got out before she could answer, and opened the door for her.

'I think that I should go back to the hospital, thank you all the same . . .'

'Why?'

She said crossly. 'Why do you ask such awkward questions? I—I just think that I should go back now.'

He took her arm and urged her across the pavement. 'Just for once allow your heart to rule your prudent common sense. What a good thing that you have decided not to marry the Reverend Joshua Watts; he would have spent the rest of his life trying to get the better of you and failing lamentably.'

She stood still, very aware of his hand on her arm. 'That's not a nice thing to say, in fact it's rude—eminent consultants shouldn't be rude!'

He laughed. 'Eminent consultants are the same as anyone else—they dislike and like, hate and love, just as they do; lose their tempers, fly into rages, forget things, speak their minds...'

'This,' said Eugenie with a snap, 'is a silly conversation to have in the middle of the pavement.'

'Indeed yes. Let us go indoors before I do something even sillier.' His voice was silky; it seemed prudent to do just that. Once inside, she told herself, she would make a few suitable remarks about the day and bid him a cool goodbye. She hoped it would be cool; she found it difficult to be that when she was with him.

Her sensible plans were flung to the four winds; as they went into the drawing-room Saphira turned away from the window to face them.

She spoke in Dutch, ignoring Eugenie. 'What were you talking about out there on the pavement? And why is she here?'

If Aderik had been surprised at seeing her, nothing of it showed on his placid face. 'Eugenie and I and Butch have been in the country, walking—a delightful day. Did you have an enjoyable time with the van Hoeves?'

'You said you had work to do.' She still spoke in Dutch. 'The moment I turn my back you're off with this girl.'

'Shall we continue our talk in English?' He spoke quietly but there was ice in his voice. 'You forget that Eugenie knows very little Dutch.'

Saphira glanced at Eugenie. 'Well, it wouldn't be worth it, would it? You'll be gone in a few days.'

Eugenie found her voice; she had felt dreadful standing there, aware that she was being talked about and unable to understand more than a word here and there. She said pleasantly while she seethed, 'Yes—how quickly the time has gone. You won't mind if I go back to the hospital? I promised to go out this evening.'

She uttered the fib with such composure that Mr Rijnma ter Salis gave her a quick look, although all he said was, 'I'll drive you back.'

'Why, thank you,' said Eugenie sweetly. Her smile was angelic, and she beamed at Saphira. 'I expect we shall see each other again before I leave.'

She kept up a cheerful chatter as he drove her back, the kind of talk she had perfected as a rector's daughter: the weather, the state of the crops, gardens and gardening, to all of which he responded with absent-minded grunts.

At the hospital he got out, opened her door and, as she went past him, put a hand on her arm.

'I apologise for Saphira, she doesn't always mean what she says. I'm sorry that she was so cross...'

'Don't give it a thought,' said Eugenie airily. 'I hope you have a happy evening together, and thank you again for my very pleasant day. I shall go back to England with some happy memories of Holland.'

'You will be glad to return?'

'Yes.' She summoned up a smile again. 'Good evening, Mr Rijnma ter Salis.'

She whisked herself into the hospital, hoping that she gave the impression that she was going somewhere with no time to waste.

In her room she sat down on the bed and allowed her thoughts to have their way. Saphira was horrible; Aderik would be unhappy with her even if he loved her. Of course, she might be quite different when they were on their own—Eugenie decided not to think too much about that. That she was to go back to England soon had been made plain; he had said nothing definite but obviously Saphira knew something about it. She must accept the truth, that he thought of her as a colleague and, since she was on foreign ground, someone to keep a friendly eye upon. Why though had he called her his love? Just the once and in stressful circumstances, she granted that—perhaps he had been filled with longing for Saphira ...

She went down to supper presently and then joined the other sisters in their sitting-room to drink coffee and watch television until it was time for bed.

She was up early the next morning and, primed by a friendly sister, hired a bike and took herself off to Den Ham—there was an old farmhouse there, she had been told, well worth a visit although it wasn't possible to go inside.

It was a pleasant outing. She had a snack lunch at a village café and cycled on to Oldehoeve and then followed the canal back to Groningen.

She had tea in Groningen, returned the bike and went back to the hospital. Two or three of the sisters had asked her to go with them to an evening concert and she had accepted gladly. The concert was in one of the churches, and when it was over they went on to a restaurant on the Sluiskade and had supper: smoked eel on buttered toast and then *pannenkoeken*—pancakes thick with crisp bacon and

served with syrup, washed down with several cups
of coffee. As she ate, Eugenie wondered what
Aderik and Saphira were eating—something much
daintier, probably; Saphira would turn up her nose
at this simple and ample supper.

It wasn't until Wednesday that she saw Mr Rijnma
ter Salis again and then only in Theatre. He wished
her good morning with easy courtesy and made
several remarks concerning the case he was to operate on, and he made no reference to their day
together. She hadn't expected him to. As usual, the
sight of him sent her heart bouncing against her
ribs and the colour to her cheeks, but since she was
masked that didn't matter and she was so well
trained that she was able to ignore her personal
feelings and concentrate upon her work.

   He went away as soon as he had finished operating and she and the Dutch theatre sister who had
scrubbed with her began on the task of getting the
theatre ready again, making sure that the nurses
were doing their work. They discussed their off-
duty as they worked, and it was then that Eugenie
learned that her replacement was due to arrive in
a few days' time. So why hadn't Mr Rijnma ter
Salis told her? she wondered. Surely she was en-
titled to know as soon as possible. She made a few
non-committal remarks to her companion and
wondered if she should go to the *directrice* and find
out for herself.

   They went to a late meal then and off duty for
the afternoon and, since it seemed that she might
expect to go back to England so soon, she decided
to shop for presents to take with her. She would go

home of course and make up her mind where she would like to work, if possible not too far from it. Certainly not London; she might meet Aderik there and she was determined to forget him once she had left Holland.

She had done her shopping—delicate little silver coffee spoons for her mother, cigars for her father—he seldom smoked them but he would enjoy having them on his desk—small presents for various friends and a pottery vase for herself, a reminder of Groningen—when she came face to face with Saphira, who to her surprise put out a hand and stopped her.

'Eugenie, how nice to see you and just as I was going to have a cup of tea—do please come with me, I do not like to have it alone.'

They were a stone's throw from the café where Eugenie had first gone and already Saphira was urging her towards it.

'I'm on duty in an hour...'

'Tea will take but half that time and the hospital is only a few minutes' walk away.'

Short of being downright rude, Eugenie could think of no way of escaping. She allowed herself to be taken into the café and settled in a chair opposite Saphira.

Saphira was being charming, talking of this and that, smiling a great deal. Eugenie wondered why. Had she decided that Eugenie was no great threat to her future or had Aderik suggested that she might be more polite? She replied suitably to Saphira's small talk and, not really trusting her one inch, braced herself against any nasty surprises.

A good thing she had; over their second cup of tea Saphira said, with every appearance of friendliness, 'Well, I have at last named a day for our marriage—mine and Aderik's.' Her blue eyes raked Eugenie's face for any sign of dismay and found none. 'I know that you will be delighted. He has pestered me for months—ever since we became engaged, but I needed time...' She sighed fearfully dramatically. 'It is after all a serious undertaking.' She gave a tinkling laugh. 'He has asked me so often to marry him and always I said wait, wait——' she paused '—and then the other day I was upset when he spent it with you, and I told him that I would not allow him to spend days with other women. He laughed, can you imagine? "I needed to do something drastic," he told me. "I needed to make you a little jealous and Eugenie was free."'

Eugenie controlled a strong desire to lean across the elegant little table and slap Saphira's face. With her feelings nicely under control she observed pleasantly, 'We had a very nice day together. I at least enjoyed it enormously and since Aderik had invited me for such a good reason I expect he found it tolerable.' She smiled. 'I find it hard to believe, though; he has never struck me as other than an honest man.'

Saphira put her cup down with some force. 'You do not believe me? Do you wish to speak to him to his face?'

'Certainly not. It is no concern of mine.' Eugenie's voice was pure sugar. 'I am sure that Aderik deserves you.' Her smile was a model of sweetness. 'I must go now or I shall be late on duty. Thank you for my tea. I dare say we shan't see each

other again; I'll be going back in a day or two—
or so I hear.'

Since it was polite to shake hands, she did so,
gripping her companion's elegantly gloved hand
hard enough to make her wince. The walk back to
the hospital was short, too short for her to shake
off her rage.

She didn't see Mr Rijnma ter Salis the next day
which was a good thing, for it gave her time to
assume a cool front. She was glad of it when Zuster
Corsma told her that her replacement would arrive
in two days' time. 'So you will return to England—
we shall miss you.'

Which from her was high praise.

There was a bypass operation the next morning.
Eugenie laid up and scrubbed and waited with her
usual calm for the surgeons to come into Theatre.
Mr Rijnma ter Salis wished her good morning,
staring at her over his mask, and she replied ser-
enely, exchanged a few words with Dr van Groot
with whom she was on the best of terms, and bent
to her work with her usual calm. It was after the
operation as he was on the point of leaving Theatre
that Mr Rijnma ter Salis asked her to spare him a
few minutes.

She followed him to Zuster Corsma's office and
was glad to see that that lady was there, looking as
though she intended to stay. Her hopes were dashed
though. Zuster Corsma muttered something to him
and went away, leaving them facing each other.

'You are to return home on the day after
tomorrow, Eugenie.'

She met his eyes. She said airily, 'Oh, I know—
I was told a day or two ago.'

'I should have told you myself but I have had very little time. I wonder if you would like to stay a few days longer; see more of Groningen, perhaps visit den Haag and Leeuwarden? It could be arranged.'

'In the same way as you arranged our day together? No, thank you!'

'What do you mean by that?' He was staring at her with hard blue eyes.

'I meant exactly what I said—I usually do.' She suddenly lost her temper. 'You ought to be ashamed of yourself, making use of me like that. If you had told me why in the first place I might not have minded as much.'

'I don't think I know what you are talking about.' His voice was hard.

'Oh, go on with you!' said Eugenie, thoroughly put out. 'I thought that we were friends after a fashion but we're not, are we? And I mind very much being used——'

He caught her by the shoulders. 'You're talking nonsense. It is a pity that I haven't time to get to the bottom of this rigmarole, Eugenie——'

'Don't you "Eugenie" me. Go away, do. I never want to see you again.'

A fiery speech rather spoilt by his nasty laugh. 'How unfortunate if there should be a patient who needs surgery before you leave.'

'Pooh!' said Eugenie and turned her back.

She wouldn't cry, she told herself when he had gone. Besides, there wasn't time—Zuster Corsma would be back.

There was an emergency early the next morning, a man who had been shot at in a bank raid and had pellets in his heart. Mr Rijnma ter Salis, looking as though four o'clock in the morning was his usual hour at which to start work, greeted her with cold politeness, operated at length, and thanked her as he left the theatre. She didn't see him again although on the following day he watched from a window as she got into the taxi which would take her to the airport.

# CHAPTER EIGHT

EUGENIE went into London from Heathrow and caught a train to Exeter. Matt would meet her there and drive her home. She saw him waiting for her on the platform and some of her unhappiness was swept away at the sight of his kind face. He saw her into the car, put her luggage in the boot and got in beside her.

'Had a good time?' he wanted to know.

It took the whole journey telling him where she had been and what she had done but never once did she mention Mr Rijnma ter Salis, and if Matt found that strange he said nothing.

Her mother and father and Tiger and Smarty were in the porch waiting for her. Matt, pressed to come in and have a drink, shook his head. 'Reckon you'll have plenty to say to each other,' he chuckled. 'I'll be up tomorrow evening, Reverend, same as usual. I'll have it then.'

They sat down to supper presently after the presents had been handed out and Eugenie had been up to her room with her case. It was a leisurely meal and Eugenie told them exactly what she had decided to tell them, barely mentioning Mr Rijnma ter Salis's name and skating lightly over their outings together.

It was much later, as her parents got ready for bed, that her mother observed, 'Eugenie hardly mentioned Aderik—I wonder why?'

'Probably because she saw little of him other than when they were in the operating theatre, my dear.'

Mrs Spencer finished plaiting her hair and tied it with a pink bow. Her dear daughter wasn't happy despite her bright chatter that evening, but it was a waste of time convincing her father of that. He would merely tell her in his gentle way not to be fanciful.

Eugenie was up early. The moor stretched away into an early morning mist and looking at it from her window wasn't enough. She went quietly downstairs, made tea, fed Smarty and, accompanied by Tiger, went out into the morning. It was fresh but it was going to be a warm day; it was just right for a brisk walk. She set out, with Tiger lolloping to and fro ignoring the sheep and the lambs moving slowly about cropping the grass.

It was a splendid opportunity to think, she told herself, and not about Aderik—a week or so at home and then another job, but where? Not too far from home; her father was well again but there was always the chance that he would have another attack. The Reverend Mr Watts had gone but there would be someone else to take his place if her father should fall ill again. It would have to be somewhere she could come home for her days off each week so that she could keep an eye on him. Well, there were several possibilities—Exeter, Bristol, Plymouth—each with large modern hospitals. Theatre jobs weren't so easy to get but she could try for a surgical ward... She viewed the prospect with gloom, her normal good spirits quite doused by the future unfolding before her. A future without

Aderik, and if she couldn't be his wife she didn't want to be anyone else's.

She was no more certain what she wanted to do by the time she got home again, but the walk had done her good. The lovely vastness of the moor had calmed her, and she presented a cheerful face at the breakfast table. She listened to her father's suggestions as to what she might do while she was at home, agreed cheerfully to them and observed that at the end of a week she would start looking for a job.

The week went quickly. Helping her mother around the house, visiting parishioners for her father, helping with the Sunday school, driving her mother into Ashburton to shop—there was more than enough to keep her busy but still there was time to think of Aderik.

True to her word, at the end of the week she studied the nursing magazines in the hope of finding something suitable. There was nothing; next week, she promised herself, if there was nothing near her home, she would put an advertisement in. She still had money, for she hadn't spent much in Holland but it wouldn't last for ever and she had no intention of subbing off her father.

She had been at home for ten days when Dr Shaw called to see her father, who submitted with ill grace to an examination and then, cheered by the news that he was, considering the circumstances, a fit man once more, joined Eugenie and her mother and the doctor for coffee.

'What do you intend to do?' asked Dr Shaw of Eugenie.

'Well, there is nothing in this part of the world at the moment. I don't want to go too far away from home—it's nice to come back for days off.'

'You wouldn't be interested in a job as nurse to a private consultant in Torquay? Not quite up to your level but very handy for coming home. He's a busy man—a surgeon—mostly general surgery. Rather peppery, I believe, but very well liked by his patients.'

'Do you know him?'

'Oh, yes. I've met him several times. A good man. As I said, not quite your cup of tea, Eugenie, but you could try it for a few months.'

'How do I find out more about him?'

Dr Shaw got up to go. 'Write and offer to take on the job—mention me if you like and go and see him.'

It would make a change; somehow she had been dreading going back to hospital. 'I'll do that. Thank you for telling me about it. Has it been advertised?'

'No, no. He mentioned it to me when I saw him last week.'

Which wasn't quite true, but he wasn't going into the telephone calls and letters which had passed between himself, Mr Sawyer in Torquay and Mr Sawyer's old friend Mr Rijnma ter Salis. If the latter was anxious to see that Eugenie found work to her liking as soon as possible, and near her home, he saw no reason to argue the matter. Mr Sawyer seemed quite content with the arrangement and it would be most suitable for Eugenie, whom he liked.

'Drop him a line,' he advised.

She did and, given an appointment a few days ahead, she drove herself down to Torquay. The fine

weather had continued for almost a week now and
the town looked at its best under a blue sky. The
holiday season was in full swing now and the streets
were crowded. Eugenie drove into the town and then
away from the sea into a broad avenue lined with
trees and, behind those, substantial houses, solid
and Victorian red brick, their paintwork pristine.
There were brass plates beside several of their solid
front doors and she drove slowly now, looking for
the right house. It was detached and slightly larger
than its neighbours. She parked the car tidily,
walked up the short tiled path and rang the bell.

She was admitted by an elderly woman in an
overall, led to a small waiting-room and told to sit
down. The room was empty but, unlike most
waiting-rooms, pleasant enough. What was more,
the magazines tidily stacked on the centre table were
almost up-to-date, there were flowers on the shelf
of books and there was wall-to-wall carpeting. She
wondered what kind of a man Mr Sawyer might
be...

He was not what she had expected. When she
was ushered into his consulting-room presently he
rose from behind his desk to shake her hand, a
short, stout man with a walrus moustache, gingery
hair going very thin on top and pale blue eyes under
heavy brows. His face was round and smiling and
she had the feeling that any minute now he might
start a song and dance act...

He had a strong grip and a rich deep voice. 'Miss
Eugenie Spencer—recommended to me by our good
Dr Shaw. Sit down, do, while we have a little talk.
I have your letter and references here some-
where...' He tossed over the piles of papers on his

desk. 'Can't find them for the moment, not that it matters, they were quite satisfactory. When can you start?'

She hadn't expected that. Before she could answer he went on, 'My nurse is leaving at the end of the week—getting married.' He put on a pair of old-fashioned spectacles and peered at her over them. 'You're very pretty—I suppose you'll do that too.'

'I have no plans to marry, Mr Sawyer, I can come as soon as you want me to. If I could know a little more about the job?'

'Splendid. Come on Saturday morning and settle in. I see patients between nine and ten o'clock each morning, go to hospital until one or two o'clock, come back here and see more patients. Quite often I have the odd patient in the evening. Half day for you on Thursday—I have out-patients' clinic at the hospital then—half-day Saturday and all Sunday. You can go home. Got a car, have you?'

'Yes, yes, I have. Shall I be able to take over your nurse's rooms or wherever she is living?'

'She lives with her mother, but she knows of someone...' He rustled through the papers again and came up with a crumpled piece of paper. 'Mrs Brewer, lives round the corner over the paper shop. Glad to have a lodger. You'd better go and see her before you go back. Did I tell you your salary? No?' He mentioned what she considered to be a very fair amount. 'I'll put it all in writing. No contract, a month's notice on either side unless something crops up.'

Which could mean anything.

They parted the best of friends, she to go and find Mrs Brewer and he to telephone his old friend Aderik Rijnma ter Salis.

There was a side door by the paper shop with a steep staircase beyond. Eugenie climbed it, knocked on the door at its head and was admitted by a wispy little woman holding a large tabby cat in her arms.

'You'll be the young lady from Mr Sawyer—come on in. I was expecting you.' She smiled uncertainly. 'It's a nice room and you can have your breakfast and supper.' She led the way down a narrow hall and into a room at its end. It was small, certainly, but it had a large window overlooking a neglected garden and it was nicely furnished and very clean.

Eugenie enquired the rent and said she would like to come as a lodger.

'Suits me,' said Mrs Brewer. 'You can have a key but no followers, mind, I won't have young men in and out at all hours.'

'I haven't any followers,' said Eugenie mildly.

'Well, you ought to have—pretty as a picture you are and no mistake.'

Eugenie drove herself back home, speculations as to her new job interlarded with thoughts of Aderik. Once she was working again, she told herself, she would forget him, but until then there was no harm in going over every moment they had been together, the things he had said, her regrettable loss of temper. It would have been nice if they had parted as good friends. 'Water under the bridge,' said Eugenie loudly, and drove thankfully through the village and up the lane to her home.

Her parents were pleased. 'It's nice that you'll be coming home at the weekends,' observed her mother, and her father looked up to say, 'You will be able to take Sunday school again, my dear.'

She agreed cheerfully. She was going to have to fill the gap made by Aderik's going; Sunday school would help.

She wouldn't need many clothes; she drove to Ashburton and bought white nylon uniform dresses, sensible shoes and a couple of paperbacks. The evenings might be a little long. On her half-day she would go into town and buy wool and needles and any small thing to make the room more her own. She had a small radio; a few flowers and books and the place would be quite cosy. She packed, took Tiger for a long walk early on Saturday morning, bade her parents and Smarty goodbye and then drove herself down to Torquay.

She had been asked to go to Mr Sawyer's house on Saturday afternoon when the nurse who was leaving would take her round the consulting-room, the reception desk and the small room at the back where she would make tea and coffee, file notes and sterilise any instruments which might have been used.

The nurse was pleasant and friendly. 'It's a good job,' she said. 'I've been here three years. I've been wanting to leave for months but Mr Sawyer kept asking me to stay a bit longer until suddenly, last week, he said he'd heard of a suitable nurse to take over and I could leave. I must say it was a surprise, coming so quickly, but of course I'm delighted. He's nice to work for but he gets a bit testy sometimes. Don't take any notice.'

Eugenie, peering in cupboards and drawers and inspecting the shelves of patients' notes, said that she wouldn't.

She had brought flowers from the garden with her, and by the time that she had got out her one or two photographs, filled a couple of vases and unpacked, her room at Mrs Brewer's looked quite comfortable. There was a small gas fire, a gas ring and a washbasin and she could use a bathroom before eight o'clock in the morning and after nine o'clock at night. She was free to go to the kitchen if she wanted to make herself a drink. She ate her supper in the bright little kitchen, with Mrs Brewer sharing out lamb chops and vegetables equally between them while the tabby cat sat at her feet.

'Mopsy is partial to a nice bit of lamb,' said Mrs Brewer, and nodded with approval as Eugenie took the hint and set aside some of her chop for Mopsy's benefit.

'Mind you,' said Mrs Brewer, 'I'll not be having my supper with you in the evenings. I like to eat in the middle of the day. You let me know when you come back of an evening and I'll cook your supper then. Have it on a tray in your room. Breakfast I'll be here—got to be there at half-past eight o'clock sharp, so breakfast will be at eight punctual. 'I go to bingo twice a week so your supper'll be in the oven.' She added, 'You're welcome to sit in the front room of an evening. I've got the telly.'

Eugenie went for a brisk walk along the sea-front the next day, ate a snack lunch at a crowded little café close by and thought with longing of Dartmoor.

She was glad when it was Monday morning and she could go to the consulting-rooms. There was a part-time receptionist, a Miss Parkes, who could have been any age between forty and sixty. She had a faintly disapproving air about her, a thin sharp nose and a staid skirt and blouse. Eugenie sensed that Miss Parkes wasn't going to like her, although she had no idea why. She replied politely to Miss Parkes's few remarks and went about her duties until Mr Sawyer arrived and the morning's work started.

She brushed through the first day quite well, no thanks to Miss Parkes who forbore to give helpful advice or hints which might have made her work easier. Mr Sawyer, unless he was in a peppery mood, was easy to work for. He was obviously liked by his patients, and when the last one had gone he had his coffee while he telephoned, dictated a letter or two, told her what to prepare for the afternoon's patients and suggested that if she had any time to spare she might like to tidy his desk.

This surprised her so much that she stared at him for a moment until he said gruffly, 'Yes, I know, we usually work in a muddle, don't we? But there are some notes somewhere—I haven't time to look for them—Mr Harry Dawes and Mrs J.B. Weatherby—they'll be coming this afternoon so be a good girl and find them.'

She had sorted the papers tidily by the time he came back, and the notes he wanted were laid in the centre of his desk where he couldn't possibly miss them. He was late and she had spent half an hour assuring his first patient that he would come as soon as he possibly could.

He sat himself down at his desk, and she saw his tired face. 'I'll bring you a cup of coffee—you've missed lunch, sir?'

'An appendix—bust while I was operating—held us up.'

'You've had no lunch?'

'No. Is Mrs Weatherby here?'

'Yes, in the waiting-room. Five minutes more won't matter—I'll cut you a sandwich.'

He nodded thankfully, reflecting that Aderik was right. She wasn't only beautiful, she was sensible and composed and didn't waste time dilly-dallying around.

He drank his coffee and ate the cheese sandwich and asked her to bring in the first patient.

The week went quickly. Eugenie found the work pleasant and far less taxing than theatre work; only the evenings were lonely. She had gone for a walk on the first evening but the town was crowded with visitors and she had quickly discovered that she was considered fair game by any man on the look-out for a companion. So she ate her supper on a tray in her room when Mrs Brewer was home and, when she was playing bingo, in the kitchen with the tabby cat for company.

On her half day she had bought wool and needles and started on socks for her father, ready for the winter, and she read a great deal. After that first day she got up early and went for a quick walk before her breakfast. It was pleasant then; the streets were quiet and there was no one about except milkmen and postmen. During her lunch hour she bought sandwiches and a carton of milk and went to a small public garden not too far away. Miss

Parkes stayed where she was, eating her lunch and drinking the tea she made for herself. Eugenie would have had her lunch with her if she had been asked, but Miss Parkes had been quick to tell her that the other nurse had always gone home at lunchtime.

It was after one o'clock on Saturday by the time she had cleared up and was ready to leave the consulting-rooms. She hurried back to Mrs Brewer's, changed into a cotton dress, slung her shoulder-bag, caught up her purse and went down to the car, parked handily in the clearing by the shop, and without wasting a moment she drove herself home.

Her heart gave a leap of pure pleasure as she drove out of Ashburton towards the moor, and presently on to the narrow ribbon of road running between the great stretches of moor. The village was quiet in the afternoon sun, but they must have heard her coming up the hill for her parents, as well as Tiger and Smarty, were waiting at the open door.

Presently her mother said, 'We'll have tea outside, shall we? Take your things upstairs, dear, while I boil the kettle. Oh, and there's a letter for you. I put it on the hall table. It's from Holland.'

Eugenie flew back into the hall, suddenly pale. Aderik. He'd written, perhaps he was coming, a dozen absurd thoughts rushed through her head. She picked up the letter and saw at once that it was from Zuster Corsma.

Her disappointment was so great that she could have burst into tears, which, she told herself a moment later, was ridiculous. Why should he write to her anyway? And how could she have been so silly as to imagine he would? He'd probably for-

gotten her already. She went back slowly with the
letter in her hand.

'It's from the theatre sister at Groningen. I'll read
it presently.'

She spoke so brightly that her mother gave her
a second glance and guessed with maternal instinct
that it hadn't been the letter Eugenie had hoped
for. Come to think of it, her dear daughter hadn't
been quite herself since she had come back from
Holland. Oh, as cheerful as always, but prone to
fall into long silences ... She's in love, decided Mrs
Spencer, and it'll be Aderik. So why isn't he in love
with her?

She set about finding out, taking her time about
it over the weekend, but Eugenie wasn't forth-
coming. She evaded her mother's cunningly put
questions while at the same time providing her with
a great deal of detailed information about the hospital, the people in it and the sights to be seen there.
She enlarged on Madeira too but she had little to
say about Bosnia, simply because it was difficult
to talk about that without mentioning Aderik.

She drove herself back on Sunday evening with
the promise that she would be back again the following weekend, and found Mrs Brewer out and a
note on the kitchen table. There was cold meat and
salad in the fridge and a tea-tray set ready; she could
make coffee if she preferred.

She ate her supper in the kitchen, listening to the
radio and feeding the cat with most of the meat.
She wasn't hungry and he obviously was.

The week went slowly despite the fact that Mr
Sawyer had a great many patients, overflowing into
the evening and presenting all kinds of compli-

cations which necessitated a lot of telephoning, soothing cups of tea and coffee and dealing sympathetically with apprehensive relations who had accompanied the patients. Mr Sawyer, while showing the greatest patience towards them, became a little testy towards the end of the week and she could hardly blame him, for he had his work at the hospital as well. On the whole she was glad to have her days filled. Miss Parkes remained faintly disapproving and, although doing her own work meticulously, she never once offered to do anything other than that, not even to put the kettle on when there was a moment free for a cup of tea. It didn't matter, Eugenie told herself; she was lucky to have a job so near home and compared with theatre work it was undemanding. All the same, by Friday afternoon she longed for Saturday. There would be patients in the morning but after that she would be free. A long walk on the moor with Tiger for company—and her thoughts, of course.

She was late leaving the consulting-rooms and Mrs Brewer greeted her from the kitchen door as she went in. 'Your supper's ready. A bit late, aren't you?'

'It's been a busy week—I'll be down for my tray in a minute, Mrs Brewer.'

She would have liked a few minutes to sit and do nothing but she didn't want to annoy her landlady; she was a good soul but fussy...

It was sausages, spinach and potatoes, with prunes and custard for pudding. Good wholesome food, she told herself, putting the kettle on the gas ring for coffee. She wasn't hungry but she was a sensible girl and she began on the sausages and, since she hadn't thought about Aderik all day, she thought about him now.

She was aroused from this by the murmur of voices and then Mrs Brewer tapping on the door and opening it. 'I said no followers, Miss Spencer, and I meant it, but seeing as this gentleman is a medical man and a friend of Mr Sawyer, I'll say no more.'

She stood aside to let Mr Rijnma ter Salis ease his vast person past her.

Eugenie, a sausage-laden fork halfway to her mouth, allowed a held breath to escape. 'I don't have followers, Mrs Brewer.' Her voice wasn't quite steady. Her eyes were on Aderik's face, which was calm and faintly amused.

'I appreciate your kindness, Mrs Brewer,' he said smoothly. 'Miss Spencer and I have worked together and it seemed a splendid opportunity to look her up while I am in England.'

Mrs Brewer nodded. 'Since you're a doctor...' She closed the door behind her as she went, and he walked further into the room.

'Good evening, Mr Rijnma ter Salis,' said Eugenie, which sounded silly but was all she could think of to say.

'Good evening to you, Miss Eugenie Spencer. A pleasant one too, is it not? But I'm not here to discuss the weather.'

She abandoned the sausage. 'Why are you here?'

'I wanted to be sure that you were happy. May I sit down?'

She flushed. 'I'm sorry, please do. I'm very happy, thank you.' She put the tray to one side. 'Are you at the hospital here?'

'No, no. George Sawyer is an old friend of mine and I just had a couple of days free.'

'Oh, I see. You're staying with him.'

'No.'

'Then how did you know that I was here? I suppose he happened to mention my name.'

'No need. I already knew where you were.'

She looked at him then. 'You did? But how . . . ?' She sat up very straight. 'This job—did you arrange it? Did you? Get him to take me on—was it just to ease your conscience?' She had gone pale with rage.

He ignored the rage. 'Yes, it was I who suggested you. He mentioned that he was looking for a nurse. No, let us be quite truthful with each other, I asked him if he knew of a suitable job for you and he told me that he was looking for a nurse.' He smiled at her. 'You see, I wanted you to be somewhere where I could hear of you from time to time.'

She pondered an answer to this and couldn't find one. 'Would you like some coffee?' she asked finally. 'And then I think you had better go.'

She picked up a spoon and stirred the prunes and custard round and round. It looked so unappetising that she put the spoon down again.

'I thought we might have dinner together. If we could hide that food on the tray.'

She had got over her surprise by now. 'Thank you, no. I have my supper here——' she took care not to look at the tray '—and I really have no wish to go out with you. Indeed, I have no wish to see you again—ever!'

He got up. 'In that case, I'll say goodbye, Eugenie.' He smiled—not a nice smile, she noticed—and went to the door. 'Enjoy those sausages!' he observed, 'and while you eat them reflect upon the fact that I am not the Reverend Mr Watts, to be rolled up and dismissed with ladylike venom.'

She gaped at him and then words came tumbling on to her tongue. Too late, he had gone.

She had no intention of crying, she told herself, and poured a cup of coffee, turning her back on the sausages. She was hungry, but not as hungry as all that. Presently she heard Mrs Brewer's plodding feet and then a tap on the door. She just had time to pick up her knife and fork before the door opened.

'He's gone,' said Mrs Brewer unnecessarily. 'Worked for him, did you? One of them clever doctors, I dare say, knows what's what. Quite agreed with me that I couldn't have followers in the house. Well, seeing as he's gone, I'll go down to the hall—there's bingo and I've a fancy for a game or two.' She paused at the door. 'Lock the door if you go to bed—I won't be back much before half-past ten.'

Eugenie made play with her knife and fork, wished her landlady a pleasant evening and waited until she heard the front door close. Then she skipped downstairs with her tray, put her uneaten supper into a plastic bag and went back for her jacket and purse. There was a fish and chip shop five minutes' walk away and, although her heart was breaking, she was hungry now. She would have to eat it there—Mrs Brewer's sharp nose would detect the smell of fish the moment she got back and that might be awkward...

She waited another ten minutes or so, in case Mrs Brewer had forgotten something, and then let herself out of the house.

Mr Rijnma ter Salis was standing beside the door, leaning against the wall. He took her arm and marched her briskly along the road.

'I've been looking around—there's a café in the next road—Kate's Kitchen or Olive's Oven or something as unlikely—it looks all right—we can have a meal there.'

'Are you mad?' demanded Eugenie tartly, doing her best to disentangle her arm.

'No, no, neither am I the Reverend Mr Watts.'

'Stop talking about him all the time, do,' said Eugenie, being hurried along round the corner towards the café—Bella's Bakery, 'and how dare you pester me like this?'

'You were going to get fish and chips, were you not?' he asked placidly. 'Mrs Brewer's feelings would have been hurt.'

She stopped short. 'Oh, I left the bag on the kitchen table...'

'Your supper? Let me have it when we go back. I'll get rid of it.'

They had reached the café and he opened the door, but she paused. 'I meant what I said,' she told him steadily.

'Yes, I know you did. I'm hungry too—shall we bury the hatchet while we eat? You don't need to talk, indeed forget I'm here. Besides, there isn't all that much time to chat. When is Mrs Brewer coming back?'

He had sat her down at a table in the window in the half-empty little place. She said, 'About half-past ten, but she might come back earlier.'

'In that case we shall have to invent something on the spot, but I should think we'd be safe for an hour.'

A middle-aged woman in a cretonne overall came to take their order. She had a refined voice and gave the impression that she was doing a job far beneath her social status. 'The chicken's off, so is the plaice—there's sausages or omelettes.'

'An omelette, please,' said Eugenie, 'and salad.'

'Ham omelette and chips and peas—what will you drink, Eugenie?'

'Only soft drinks,' said the waitress sternly.

They decided on lemon squash and, cross though she was, Eugenie had a job not to smile at his pained expression when he drank it.

The omelettes were surprisingly good; Eugenie refused a pudding but accepted a cup of coffee, and while she drank it mentally framed several polite expressions of thanks for her meal.

'Don't waste time on thinking up polite thank-yous,' said Mr Rijnma ter Salis kindly. 'They'll be quite wasted on me anyway. If you're ready we'll go back and you can give me the bag.'

He was so matter-of-fact that she felt offended. After all, it was she who should be off-hand. While they walked back to the paper shop she was silent, annoyance and ill temper giving way to a sadness that he was treating her so casually. He really had come just to see if she had a job and for no other reason—she didn't specify to herself what other reason there might be.

She gave him the key and they went upstairs and into the kitchen and she handed him the plastic bag. 'Thank you for my supper and for getting rid of this. I hope you have a pleasant time in England.' On an impulse she added, 'I hope Saphira is well.'

'In the very best of spirits.'

She didn't want him to go, and this time it would be final; he had satisfied himself that she was settled in a job, and now he could go back to Groningen and get married. If he didn't go quickly she was going to burst into tears...

She said goodbye and then went to the door and held it open. If he said *tot ziens* then she might see him again, for that was what it meant. He said casually, 'Goodbye, Eugenie,' and took the bag and walked away.

The tabby cat was sitting in front of the fridge in a suggestive manner and she got out his cat food and put a dollop in his saucer. Tears were trickling down her cheeks and she wiped them away with her fingers and went upstairs. She would have taken Mopsy with her for company, but Mrs Brewer wouldn't allow that. She had a bath, still weeping and not caring, for it was a suitable place in which to have a good cry, and then she got into bed and closed her eyes. 'You've been a fool, my girl,' she muttered, 'and there's to be no more of this nonsense!'

All the same she allowed herself a few moments in which to think about Aderik before she went to sleep.

# CHAPTER NINE

EUGENIE had supposed that as the weeks went by Aderik's image would fade. It did no such thing. She thought about him all the time, and even when she thrust him to the back of her head he was still there. It was unsettling, and she began to think seriously of altering her whole way of life in the hope of forgetting him. If she had been free to do so she would have found a job somewhere miles away—Australia or Canada or the remoter parts of South America, although she wasn't sure about the hospitals there—she could forget him then in a totally different environment. However, that would mean leaving her mother and father—they would never stand in her way but she couldn't leave them, and what would it be like not being able to go back to Dartmoor from time to time? The future didn't bear thinking about.

Mr Rijnma ter Salis, on the other hand, knew exactly what he was going to do with his future. It needed patience and planning, of course, and he was capable of both. He returned to Groningen and became immersed in his work to the exclusion of everything else, and when Saphira complained that he was never free to take her out to dine and dance or visit the theatre he told her that his work came first. 'I know how irksome it is for you,' he explained sympathetically, 'but you must have realised when we became engaged that I have little time for the social life you lead.'

'When we marry you will have to change that.' Saphira spoke sharply. 'I refuse to go out without you to escort me. The very idea! Let someone else do your work...'

'You don't mean that?' He looked at her curiously.

'Of course I do. You're successful and wealthy. You could still be a consultant and take private patients. That would leave you with some leisure to enjoy life.'

'I enjoy life now. It is true that when we marry I should like more time to spend at home with you and the children.'

'I don't intend to be bothered with children for the first five or six years. However good a nanny is, they're still a bother.' She smiled at him—she was a very pretty woman and her smile was charming. 'Besides, I think that a son will be all that we shall want.'

Mr Rijnma ter Salis examined the nails of one hand. 'You know I have always liked the idea of a large family——'

Saphira shouted at him then. 'Why have I just discovered what you really are? A selfish man who wants his own way. There's something more to life than work and hordes of children, and I intend to enjoy myself...' She broke off at the look of calm indifference on his face. 'Dear Aderik, see how you have made me lose my temper.' Her smile was as charming as ever. 'You must see it from my point of view. I'm young and pretty and I like a good time, and you want to bury me alive with evenings at home waiting for you to return from the hospital and children screaming their heads off. You wouldn't want to make me unhappy, would you?'

'That is the last thing I would wish to do.' He spoke quietly.

Her smile held triumph. 'Well, then, start now by taking me out to dinner.'

The phone interrupted her and he crossed the room to answer it.

'I'm wanted at the hospital,' he told her quietly, 'I have to go. Shall I drop you off or shall Jaap call a taxi?'

She had said angrily, 'A taxi. Piet van Twist will be glad to take me out to dinner.'

The week after that he had gone to Rome and after that to London. He had not gone to see Eugenie. He wanted her for his wife, but he was willing to wait. He knew that Saphira, faced with the reality of being a surgeon's wife, would never marry him, but he had to be sure of Eugenie. She was a proud piece and, although he didn't believe her when she said that she never wished to see him again, he had to be quite sure...

He had been back in Groningen less than a week when he flew to northern Italy to a hospital where refugees were being sent. He was there for several days and when he got back to his home at last, Saphira came to see him. When he had got home he had showered and changed, taken a delighted Butch into the garden and then gone to his study to read the pile of letters on his desk. He was tired and he wished very much that Eugenie were there so that he could talk to her, discuss his patients, mull over some new technique. When he had first met Saphira she had professed an interest in his work, but after they became engaged she had told him laughingly that he should forget his work when she was with him. 'To tell the truth,' she had said charmingly, 'I hate unpleasant things and there is so much fun and amusement for us to enjoy.'

Because he had fancied himself in love with her then, he had taken care not to mention anything to do with his work to her. It took only a few months for him to realise that he hadn't been in love at all and certainly he didn't love her, but it wasn't until he had seen Eugenie's lovely face looming out of the mist and listened to her unaffected voice that he knew that she was the girl he had long ago given up seeking. He had however engaged himself to Saphira, who professed to love him, and he was an honourable man. It wasn't until recently that he had realised that Saphira had begun to make demands about their future. She didn't wish to live in Groningen—a country house, not too far from the city, so that she could see her friends and they could visit at weekends. Trips to Paris and the south of France, and he should give up most of his hospital work and refuse to go all over Europe at everyone's beck and call unless the patient were someone really important. He could keep his private patients, of course...

None of these things had she demanded outright, only gently suggested them whenever they were together, a hint here and a hint there. She had been angry the last time they had seen each other, betraying her real feelings and then doing her best to hide them when she saw that she had gone too far. This man—Piet van Twist—was well-to-do, good-looking and apparently rich enough to live as he liked. Saphira had mentioned him several times lately...

It was as he sat there that Saphira came. She pushed past Jaap and sat down in the chair opposite his desk. 'So you're back!' She studied his face. 'You look tired—you will be an old man before you know where you are, Aderik. Kill yourself, most likely. What is it that they say in English? All work and no play makes Jack a dull boy! You are certainly dull, my dear.' She looked at him again and gave an uneasy laugh. 'I thought we might have a talk; there are things I want to say. Perhaps I should have said them weeks ago. We aren't suited, Aderik. Oh, we're a handsome couple and you have a nice home—two in fact with that place buried in the country—enough money to allow me to live as I like, only I wouldn't be able to do that, would I? Life with you would be so dull...' She paused and looked at him, meeting his steady gaze and dropping her eyes after a moment. 'To tell you the truth,' she declared rather loudly, 'I should be bored to death if I were to marry you.'

Mr Rijnma ter Salis spoke quietly. He sounded quite pleasant too. 'In that case, Saphira, I would be the last person to hold you to your promise. I'm sure that you will find a man who can give you the sort of life you wish for.'

'Oh, I have—Piet van Twist—he's mad about me.' She added shrewdly, 'You never were, were you?'

'I see now that I was entirely unsuitable as your husband, Saphira. I'm glad to know that you will have a happy future.'

'Oh, I shall, make no mistake about that. And you will go on working round the clock, I suppose. All the future I can see for you is a very dull one.'

Mr Rijnma ter Salis, who knew better, agreed placidly.

'Please keep the ring,' he begged her. It was a large diamond, which she had preferred to the old-fashioned rose diamond and sapphire ring which was a family heirloom.

She got up, and he stood up and came round the desk. 'I'm going to den Haag for the weekend, Aderik. You'll see to a notice in the papers, will you? I dare say we'll see each other from time to time.'

'Of course. I wish you every happiness, Saphira.' He bent and kissed her cheek and went with her to the house door. 'You're not walking? Can I drive you home?'

'Piet's waiting in the garage at the end of the street. Goodbye, Aderik.'

He was no longer tired. Presently he ate a splendid meal under Jaap's watchful eye and, unable to stay in the house, walked the streets of Groningen with Butch beside him. Jaap came into the hall as he returned home.

'A tray of coffee before you go to bed, sir—you'll be tired?'

'Tired, not in the least, but coffee would be welcome.'

Jaap went to the kitchen for it. 'The master must have had a bit of good news,' he confided. 'Ever so cheerful, he is. Let's hope he's not getting married after all, at least not to Juffrouw.' He paused. 'That English girl who came to work here——' he beamed at the idea '—now there is a young lady who would do very nicely.'

'Gone back to England,' said Meintje, 'more's the pity.'

'Love finds a way,' observed Jaap. Even in Dutch the meaning was the same.

Aderik, unaware of his faithful servant's forecast as to his future, allowed his clever head to relinquish its normal learned thoughts and daydream.

Eugenie wasn't unhappy in her job. Miss Parkes remained aloof, her manner suggesting that Eugenie was to be tolerated in a ladylike way but only because there was no alternative to that. However Mr Sawyer, despite his peppery moments, was nice to work for. He had a large practice and she was kept busy so that she had little time to feel sorry for herself. Only sometimes in the evenings she wished very much to be back on Dartmoor with Aderik there too. At least she was able to go home each weekend, teaching Sunday school, driving her father to one of the other parishes when occasion demanded, taking Tiger for a walk. It was a splendid summer and the early mornings were a delight. She wandered for an hour before breakfast, not wishing to lie awake with her thoughts, and then spent her morning at church before helping her mother with lunch. 'Keeping her hand in,' her father had laughingly declared, adding that she would make a good parson's wife.

The weekend had come round again and she drove home in the early afternoon. The morning had been busy but now she was free until Monday, her head full of plans. There would be time to drive

her mother to Buckfastleigh or Ashburton if she
wanted to do some shopping, then tea and a walk
before supper. Sunday never varied but on Monday
morning she would have time to load the washing
machine before she left, for Mr Sawyer had told
her not to go to the consulting-room until eleven
o'clock since he wouldn't be there himself before
noon.

Satisfied with her plans, she ran the car round
the side of the house and went in through the
kitchen door. Her mother was there, cutting
sandwiches.

'Darling, I didn't hear the car.' She lifted her face
for Eugenie's kiss.

'Would you like to do any shopping? There's still
plenty of time...' Her eyes fell on the plate of
sandwiches. 'Is someone coming to tea?'

'Well, not exactly,' said Mrs Spencer in a re-
signed voice. 'Joshua Watts has come to see how
your father is and I'm afraid he expects to stay the
night.'

'Mother, no... Why couldn't he have come
during the week? He's not staying long, is he?'

'No, dear, just for tonight. He wants to stay for
the morning service and go after lunch. Well, actually he said during the late afternoon so I suppose
that means tea as well.'

Mrs Spencer eyed Eugenie's cross face. 'Be nice,
darling, and don't let him upset your father.'

'He'd better not. Isn't there a whist drive or
something we can send him to this evening?'

'No, love. In this splendid weather everyone's out
of doors—we shan't start bingo or whist in the hall
until the autumn.'

Eugenie had thrown down her bag and was spreading gentleman's relish on to the slices of bread and butter. 'I'll leave the crusts on,' she said, slapping them together and cutting them briskly into triangles, 'he's got his own teeth.'

Her mother giggled. 'Darling, don't be cross. I know it's a disappointment but it's only for a day.'

'Luckily I'm not to go back until Monday morning—Mr Sawyer's away—so at least we'll have tomorrow evening.'

'Yes, dear. He's been with your father since lunch. Do you suppose you could get him away so that your father could have an hour to go over his sermon?'

'Of course, I'll take him for a walk. Tiger will like that at any rate.'

The Reverend Mr Watts rose to his feet as she went into her father's study.

'Eugenie, how delightful to see you again.' He came and shook her hand and held it for too long. She said in her matter-of-fact way, 'Hello, Joshua,' shook his hand firmly and went to kiss her father.

'Busy with your sermon? I'll take Joshua for a walk while you finish it.'

The Reverend Mr Watts was only too eager to agree to this, so she led him out through the kitchen door, whistled to Tiger in his basket, winked at her mother as she went past her and started off at a brisk pace.

'It is a warm day for walking,' observed her companion, keeping up with difficulty.

'You'll enjoy it after that stuffy place where you live.'

'Well, the fresh air is good for one, but the lack of amenities . . .'

'You mean buses and trains and rows of shops?'

He agreed eagerly. 'Yes, yes, exactly that. I am sure that if you were to live for a while in a large town or even a city you would learn to enjoy its advantages.'

'Well, I wouldn't.' She glanced at him. He was looking very earnest; she hoped he hadn't thought that she had invited him to go for a walk by way of encouragement.

It seemed that he thought she had, for he continued, 'I have a very pleasant little house, very close to the church, and there is a small park not ten minutes' walk away. I dare say that you have had time to reflect, Eugenie, and realise what a splendid future we would have together.' He stopped walking, breathing hard, whether from emotion or the rate at which they were going. '*Haec olim meminisse juvabit*,' he declared, and threw his arms wide.

'Why ever do you say that?' asked Eugenie. 'Why should it be a joy to remember today? We're only going for a walk.'

'Oh—you understand the Latin? I was prepared to translate it for you.'

'No need,' said Eugenie briskly. 'You forget that Father is by way of being a Latin scholar.'

She was setting a smart pace again and he hurried to keep up. 'Dare I hope that you have changed your mind? I am more than prepared to make you my wife . . .'

He sounded like someone out of an Edwardian novel. She mustn't hurt his feelings, though.

'You're very kind but it's quite out of the question. I don't love you, Joshua. I'm sure that before long you will meet a nice girl whom you will love and who will love you and then you'll live very happily together.'

He said thoughtfully, 'Yes, that is possible, of course. I have much to offer and I'm an ambitious man.'

'Do tell me about it,' suggested Eugenie, and had her ears filled with his ideas and plans for the rest of their walk.

In the kitchen, getting the supper ready with her mother, she told her of Joshua's renewed proposal. 'He started quoting Latin at me, Mother—that nice bit about remembering the day with joy, but he didn't mean it. I think he did it to impress me.' She sighed. 'I've had several proposals, but never one so easily forgotten as this one.'

'Well, better luck with the next one, darling!' said Mrs Spencer, and took a peep at her daughter's face. Eugenie said rather too quickly, 'Oh, but I quite like being a career girl.'

The Reverend Mr Watts went after tea on Sunday, which left very little of the weekend, but at least she was able to take a quick walk with Tiger on Monday morning, getting back to her lodgings with a few minutes to spare before she needed to leave for the consulting-rooms. Miss Parkes gave her her usual austere greeting but Mr Sawyer was positively jovial; she caught him looking at her once or twice as though he were secretly amused about something. When she brought in his coffee in between patients he asked, 'I quite forgot to say to you, did you see my old friend Aderik Rijnma ter

Salis when he came here to see me a short time ago?
You worked for him...?'

'Yes, that's right. I did see him, he called round
to Mrs Brewer's—she was annoyed, she won't allow
men in the house.'

He sugared his coffee with a heavy hand. 'Surely
she allowed him in?'

'Yes, because he was a friend of yours, sir, and
a member of the medical profession.'

'I'm glad to hear that Mrs Brewer takes such care
of her lodgers. You're comfortable there?'

'Yes, thank you.'

'You're wasted here, of course. A girl who can
work as you did in Bosnia deserves a first-rate job
in a first-rate hospital.'

'Yes, but I have to be near my parents.' She added
urgently, 'Mr Sawyer, am I not satisfactory?'

'Good Lord, yes. I didn't mean to give that impression. You're the best nurse I've had for years.
As far as I'm concerned you can stay forever. But
supposing you marry? What about your parents
then?'

'Well, I'd have to marry someone who wouldn't
mind me keeping an eye on them. I dare say he'd
be hard to find.'

'Oh, I don't know', said Mr Sawyer casually. 'Get
Mrs Symes into the dressing-room, will you? I'll
have to examine her.'

Mr Rijnma ter Salis laid his plans with the same
meticulous care that he exhibited in the operating
theatre. Being very much in love, his patience was
tried to its utmost, but since it was necessary to
wait until the weekend he went calmly on with his

work until Friday evening, when he got into his car and drove himself to Calais. There he took the hovercraft to Dover and then drove steadily through the late evening until he reached Torquay and Mr Sawyer's house.

It was late by now, but his friend had stayed up to welcome him.

'Sent the wife to bed,' said Mr Sawyer. 'A darling woman, as you know, but she'd want to chat, never mind that it's the early hours. Eugenie will be in in the morning—she should be ready to leave by noon. Goes back to Mrs Brewer, of course. Where do you intend to pick her up?'

'At Mrs Brewer's. I can park the car round the corner, out of sight.'

Mr Sawyer heaved with laughter. 'Let's hope she doesn't send you to the rightabout, Aderik.'

'She won't have the chance.'

Eugenie, intent on getting home as soon as possible, had rushed back to Mrs Brewer's, changed, and galloped down the stairs and out of the house—straight into Mr Rijnma ter Salis's elegant waistcoat. It was rather like tumbling against a tree-trunk, excepting that tree-trunks didn't have arms to wrap round one... She found her breath and pulled away from him and he dropped his arms at once.

'You,' said Eugenie, delight washing over her even while she was trying to think of something coldly scathing to say.

'Indeed it is I.' He smiled, and it wrought havoc in her heart. 'Come along, the car's over here.'

'Car? I'm driving myself home.'

He took no notice but took her arm and shovelled her gently into the Bentley, got in beside her and drove off.

'Why are you here?' Eugenie demanded. She added waspishly, 'And shouldn't Saphira be with you?'

Mr Rijnma ter Salis grinned. 'Now why should you suppose that? Saphira is, as far as I know, on holiday in the south of France, but since we are no longer engaged I have rather lost touch.'

'Not engaged? Why not? She's very suitable. Oh, dear, I do hope it's not because you quarrelled about her telling me that you wanted to make her jealous.'

'I never quarrel,' observed Mr Rijnma ter Salis placidly. 'I have known for some time that I would never marry Saphira; it was merely a question of time before she came to the same conclusion. It seems that I work too hard, refuse to go to endless parties and expect my wife to present me with a healthy brood of children.'

Eugenie had to know. 'But you loved her?'

'I was, perhaps, a little in love with her but that is quite different from loving, you know. I seldom thought of her when we were apart. I have since discovered that when one is in love one's thoughts revolve constantly around the loved one.'

'Why are you telling me all this? Didn't I say I didn't want to see you ever again?'

'I am clearing the way for what is to come.' He slowed the car and stopped on the grass verge and turned to look at her. 'And did you mean that you never wish to see me again or did you just say it? There is a difference.'

His eyes held hers. She was unable to look away from them; besides, she wasn't a good liar. 'I said it.'

The tenderness of his smile shook her but he didn't say anything, only started the car and drove on.

The silence got too much for her. 'Are you on holiday?' she asked.

'For three days, yes.' She waited for him to say something more, but since he had nothing more to say she tried again. 'Are you at the hospital in London?'

'No, I'm working in Groningen for the moment, I expect to come over here in a couple of weeks.' They were slowing down to go through Buckfastleigh. 'How do you enjoy your job now you have settled in?'

He wasn't going to talk about himself. 'I am quite content with it,' she told him and lapsed into silence again, a silence which he made no effort to break. At the Rectory he got out, opened her door and followed her to the open door where her mother was waiting. It was after she had embraced her daughter that Mrs Spencer said. 'You'll stay for lunch, Aderik? Come in do, what a lovely day, what a splendid summer we have had. Eugenie, your father's in the study. Will you tell him lunch is on the table?'

She bustled Mr Rijnma ter Salis into the sitting-room. 'Will you have a drink now or a beer with lunch?'

'Oh, the beer, thank you.'

She smiled suddenly at him. 'Everything went according to plan?'

'Just as I had hoped, Mrs Spencer. You won't mind if I go after lunch?'

She studied his quiet face. 'But you'll be back?'

'Yes—will you invite me to breakfast?'

'With pleasure, Aderik!' She turned round as Eugenie came into the room.

'I was just telling Mr Rijnma ter Salis about the beautiful sunsets we've been having,' she said airily.

He went after lunch, after saying all the right things to her parents and wishing her a casual goodbye as he got into his car. Eugenie watched him go, fighting tears, longing to gallop down the lane after him and beg him to stay. She had actually thought once or twice that morning that he had come to see her and he had said... She spent the rest of the day remembering what he had said while she pottered around the garden with her father, got tea and went along to the church to make sure that the flowers were well arranged. There were ladies enough in the village willing to do the flowers but some of them were better than others...

They didn't keep late hours at the Rectory; she was able to go to bed early, which gave her the opportunity to lie awake and have a refreshing weep. She slept towards morning and woke heavy-eyed; she was too beautiful to look plain but she certainly didn't look her best. A quick walk would set her to rights; she dressed in the first thing which came to hand—a cotton dress, faded from years of wear, and some elderly sandals. Time enough to dress for church after she returned. She crept downstairs, looked longingly at the teapot and decided not to stop for a cup of tea—she would have one when she got back, it was still only a little past six o'clock—and went out of the back door.

Mr Rijnma ter Salis rose from the upturned bucket he had perched his massive person upon, wished her a cheerful good morning and then added, just as cheerfully, 'You've been crying!'

For Eugenie, peevish after a bad night and aware that she didn't look her best, this was the last straw.

'Oh, go away, do!' She would actually have gone back indoors, only Tiger was leaning up against her expecting a walk and unwilling to move.

After a minute she asked, 'Haven't you been to bed?' which was a silly question; he looked as though he had slept all night, standing there immaculate as always, freshly shaven and not a hair of his head out of place.

He only smiled. 'Come with me?' he invited, and took her arm. 'This is the best part of the day.' He marched her off, through the garden gate and on to the moor beyond. 'I have thought many times of being here in the quiet of the early morning with you, my darling. At first it was only a dream, but dreams can come true, can they not? Although they sometimes need a little help.'

They were following a narrow path across the close-cropped grass and the sun was warm and bright. Mr Rijnma ter Salis stopped and turned her round to face him. 'I first saw you on Dartmoor and I couldn't forget you. I think you have been in my thoughts ever since that day. I'm in love with you, my dearest dear. I want you for my wife, to love and to cherish for the rest of my days.'

He wrapped his great arms around her and held her close, looking down with love on to her tousled head and her face, pale from tears and sleeplessness. She had never looked so beautiful when she smiled. 'Oh, I would so like to be cherished,' she said, 'and I'd very much like to be your wife, Aderik. I've loved you for almost all the time I've known you, I——'

He kissed her then; far more satisfactory than mere words could ever be. Presently she said, 'I would like to know——'

He caught her in a quite ruthless embrace. 'Hush, my love, can you not see that I am about to kiss you again? And that cannot wait.'

She put her arms around his neck and lifted her face to his. There would be plenty of time to talk in the happy years ahead.

# HARLEQUIN ROMANCE®

### brings you:

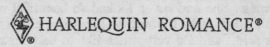

*Sealed with a Kiss*

A letter has played an important role in all our
romances in our Sealed with a Kiss series so far, and
next month's WANTED: WIFE AND MOTHER
by Barbara McMahon is no exception.

But for Caroline Evans, the letter from Australian
rancher Nick Silverman comes as something of a shock.
His letter isn't sealed with a kiss—it's a coldhearted
proposal! Nick needs a mother to take care of his little
orphaned niece, Amanda. And Caroline needs to marry to
fulfil the conditions of her great-aunt's will. A marriage of
convenience seems an ideal solution for all three of them
but, with a cynical and sexy stranger for a husband, has
Caroline taken on more than she can handle?

Don't miss Harlequin Romance #3369
*Wanted: Wife and Mother* by Barbara McMahon

Available in July wherever Harlequin books are sold.

# Take 4 bestselling love stories FREE

## Plus get a FREE surprise gift!

**Announcing
the New Pages & Privileges™ Program
from Harlequin® and Silhouette®**

### Get All This FREE
### With Just One Proof-of-Purchase!

- **FREE Travel Service** with the guaranteed lowest available airfares plus 5% cash back on every ticket

- **FREE Hotel Discounts** of up to 60% off at leading hotels in the U.S., Canada and Europe

- **FREE Petite Parfumerie** collection (a $50 Retail value)

- **FREE $25 Travel Voucher** to use on any ticket on any airline booked through our Travel Service

- **FREE Insider Tips Letter** full of fascinating information and hot sneak previews of upcoming books

- **FREE Mystery Gift** (if you enroll before June 15/95)

And there are more great gifts and benefits to come!
Enroll today and become Privileged!

(see insert for details)

**PROOF-OF-PURCHASE**

Offer expires October 31, 1996

HR-PP2